YORK NOTES

To the Lighthouse

Virginia Woolf

Note by Dr Julian Cowley

 Longman   🌼 York Press

Dr Julian Cowley is hereby identified as author of this work in accordance with
Section 77 of the Copyright, Designs and Patents Act 1988

YORK PRESS
322 Old Brompton Road, London SW5 9JH

PEARSON EDUCATION LIMITED
Edinburgh Gate, Harlow,
Essex CM20 2JE, United Kingdom
Associated companies, branches and representatives throughout the world

First published 2000

ISBN 0–582–42463–1

Designed by Vicki Pacey
Phototypeset by Gem Graphics, Trenance, Mawgan Porth, Cornwall
Colour reproduction and film output by Spectrum Colour
Produced by Addison Wesley Longman China Limited, Hong Kong

Contents

PART FOUR

TEXTUAL ANALYSIS

PART FIVE

BACKGROUND

PART SIX

CRITICAL HISTORY & BROADER PERSPECTIVES

PART ONE

INTRODUCTION

HOW TO STUDY A NOVEL

Studying a novel on your own requires self-discipline and a carefully thought-out work plan in order to be effective.

- You will need to read the novel more than once. Start by reading it quickly for pleasure, then read it slowly and thoroughly.
- On your second reading make detailed notes on the plot, characters and themes of the novel. Further readings will generate new ideas and help you to memorise the details of the story.
- Some of the characters will develop as the plot unfolds. How do your responses towards them change during the course of the novel?
- Think about how the novel is narrated. From whose point of view are events described?
- A novel may or may not present events chronologically: the time-scheme may be a key to its structure and organisation.
- What part do the settings play in the novel?
- Are words, images or incidents repeated so as to give the work a pattern? Do such patterns help you to understand the novel's themes?
- Identify what styles of language are used in the novel.
- What is the effect of the novel's ending? Is the action completed and closed, or left incomplete and open?
- Does the novel present a moral and just world?
- Cite exact sources for all quotations, whether from the text itself or from critical commentaries. Wherever possible find your own examples from the novel to back up your opinions.
- Always express your ideas in your own words.

This York Note offers an introduction to *To the Lighthouse* and cannot substitute for close reading of the text and the study of secondary sources.

Few writers have raised the novel to the status of literary art so evidently as Virginia Woolf. The refinement of her technical and formal skill has rarely been equalled, and in *To the Lighthouse*, which since its initial publication has been one of her most popular works, she was at her artistic peak.

Although it first appeared in 1927, this novel has retained its capacity to surprise readers with its innovative, yet immensely accomplished characterisation of an English family group on holiday on an island off the Scottish mainland. The surprise arises from the boldness with which Virginia Woolf focused upon the workings of the individual consciousness. Only a few simple events occur. Their importance derives from the ways in which they impinge upon the thoughts and feelings of the Ramsays and their friends. It seemed daring in 1927, and appears so today.

Although it can be seen as a novel in which little happens, it is actually a work which subtly registers immense changes. The apparently trivial details, to which Virginia Woolf pays such attention, carry the weight of a struggle to draw form out of chaos, to grant shape and meaning to human experience. The First World War reverberates, from a distance, through the heart of the novel. It forms a traumatic historical backdrop to the novelist's idiosyncratic, oblique, yet deeply moving evocation of personal loss. *To the Lighthouse* is an **elegy** for what has passed, but it is also an affirmation of human creativity. Pain and joy, and the conditions of their existence, are pressing concerns of this extraordinary novel, which perhaps explains why, for all its seriousness, it has sustained its appeal not only for literary critics, but also for a broader reading public.

PART TWO

SUMMARIES & COMMENTARIES

To the Lighthouse was published by the Hogarth Press, on 5 May 1927. Initially, 3,000 copies were printed. A second impression, of 1,000 copies, followed in June 1927; then a third impression of 1,500 in May 1928. The novel continued to sell well, and in February 1930 a further run of 3,000 appeared. An American edition of 4,000 copies was published by Harcourt, Brace and Company, also on 5 May 1927. Virginia Woolf made revisions to the initial proofs separately, so the British and the American first editions have some disparities.

This Note uses the Definitive Edition published by Vintage Books (London, 1992), which includes a list of variants between the initial editions.

SYNOPSIS

To the Lighthouse does not lend itself readily to summary. Its interest resides as much in the way it is written as in what it is about. The broad outlines of a synopsis suggest that little happens in the course of the novel, but Virginia Woolf's attention to details and to the processes of perception means that small events occur incessantly.

The novel is divided into three parts, each of which is subdivided into sections. In the first part, 'The Window', which takes place in the course of a single day, we are introduced to the Ramsay family and the guests who join them at their holiday home on the Isle of Skye.

James Ramsay, who is six years old, longs to visit a nearby lighthouse, and his mother assures him they will make the trip on the following day. His father contradicts this on the grounds that the weather will not be suitable. Mrs Ramsay is knitting a stocking.

Lily Briscoe, a younger friend of Mrs Ramsay, is positioned on the lawn, painting a picture. William Bankes, a botanist and friend of

Mr Ramsay, converses with her, and friendship develops between them. Mr Ramsay wanders around the garden, reciting poetry.

In the evening, Mrs Ramsay hosts a dinner party for her family, Lily Briscoe and William Bankes, an old poet called Augustus Carmichael and a young philosopher called Charles Tansley, and a newly engaged couple, Minta Doyle and Paul Rayley. Afterwards, Mr and Mrs Ramsay sit together reading.

In the course of the second part, 'Time Passes', ten years elapse. We learn of the death of Mrs Ramsay, and of her children Andrew and Prue. The house grows dilapidated. Eventually, an old caretaker makes preparations for the return of the Ramsays and their friends.

In the final part, 'The Lighthouse', Mr Ramsay takes his youngest children, James and Cam, to the Lighthouse. Lily Briscoe, after watching them head out to sea, completes the picture she began ten years earlier.

I THE WINDOW

Mrs Ramsay tells her son James they can visit the Lighthouse the following day. Mr Ramsay and Charles Tansley declare the trip will not be possible. Lily Briscoe stands on the edge of the lawn, painting. William Bankes stops to talk with her. Mrs Ramsay knits, and reads to James. Mr Ramsay paces around outside, reciting poetry. Around seven o'clock, his wife joins him for a stroll in the garden. Eventually, Andrew and Nancy Ramsay, Minta Doyle and Paul Rayley arrive back from their walk by the sea. A dinner party is held. Afterwards, Mrs Ramsay says goodnight to her two youngest children. Then, she and her husband sit together, reading

1

One evening, in their holiday home on the Hebridean island of Skye, north-west of the Scottish mainland, Mrs Ramsay tells her son James that they can visit the nearby Lighthouse on the following day, if the weather is fine. The six-year-old boy is filled with joy at the prospect of an expedition which he has been looking forward to for some time. As he sits in the drawing room, cutting out pictures from a catalogue of the

Army and Navy Stores he projects his own joyful feelings on to the images.

His mother, who sits knitting a stocking, watches him use the scissors, and imagines him as a judge or some other important public figure. His father, passing the drawing-room window during his evening walk on the terrace, adds his voice, declaring that the weather will not be fine. James is filled with a desire to kill this man, who seems so negative. Mrs Ramsay seeks to reassure James that all will be well.

Charles Tansley, accompanying Mr Ramsay, joins in the discussion, observing that the wind is from the west, a bad sign for the planned visit. Echoing Mr Ramsay, whom he views as a mentor, he declares there will be no visit to the Lighthouse tomorrow. Mrs Ramsay is annoyed by the insensitivity of the young man known to her children as 'the little atheist' (p. 5).

Mrs Ramsay recalls a recent occasion when she invited Tansley to accompany her to the local town. As they passed Mr Carmichael, an elderly man relaxing on the tennis lawn, she asked whether he required anything from the town. In the course of their walk, Mrs Ramsay drew Tansley's attention to a poster advertising a circus, and suggested they should all go. Tansley responded by talking of his working-class origins.

They passed through the main street to the quay, where Mrs Ramsay admired the sea, with the Lighthouse in the distance. She noted the presence of an artist, one of numerous visitors drawn to paint the scene. They stopped at the house of a poor woman and her child. Mrs Ramsay offered comfort, while Tansley waited impatiently in the parlour.

> The Lighthouse of the novel's title becomes a focus of attention immediately. It is a looming physical presence off the coast of the island, but more importantly it exists within the consciousness of individual characters. For the little boy James it is a distant goal, the object of an adventure. Virginia Woolf shows how children, who have so much less experience of living than adults, magnify the importance of such objects. The intensity of James's hostile response to his father is a measure of the strength of his desire to reach the Lighthouse (see Theme on Desire).

> Virginia Woolf portrays human character as fluid, changeable, and complex. She rejects the stock responses typical of more simplistic

forms of **realist fiction,** where a character has to react in a certain way because he or she *is* that character. Virginia Woolf was aware that an individual's response to a situation may change on account of all manner of obscure, intangible factors. She recognised that the motivation for human behaviour is rarely as obvious or straightforward as we like to think. At first we may take James's reaction to his father as evidence of the child's eccentricity, his tendency to see the world in exaggerated terms. But there are numerous other instances, throughout the novel, which undermine expectations of a simple cause-and-effect relationship between an event and the response to it (see Characterisation).

Mrs Ramsay appears an affirmative figure, optimistic in her outlook. Later in the book, her husband remarks upon her tendency to pessimism. This is neither carelessness nor wilful inconsistency on Virginia Woolf's part. Terms such as optimism and pessimism are useful to us because they are clear-cut. They allow us to make a firm distinction. Human feelings, however, rarely occur in such unalloyed form, and they are often too complex for such definitive labelling.

Mrs Ramsay's optimism about the visit to the Lighthouse is actually unrealistic. The weather does not permit the trip. Her affirmation is an effort to compensate for the world's disappointments, of which she is personally well aware. Pessimism underlies her show of optimism. Nonetheless, even a show of optimism can have positive influence in the world. As Virginia Woolf recognised, the convenient terminology we use for routine communication conceals a great deal. Her own faith in creativity was never free from fear of its opposite; the order brought about by art was affirmative, but it inevitably implied knowledge that chaos and disintegration are equally realities of life (see Theme on Art).

Virginia Woolf writes that James had looked forward to the visit 'for years and years it seemed' (p. 3). A major thematic concern of the novel is that time as experienced often seems to diverge from the span of time registered on a clock-face. Virginia Woolf was fascinated by this elasticity in our sense of time. It is something with which we are all familiar: an enjoyable experience may seem to fly past in seconds, although the clock shows that it lasted for minutes; a boring experience may appear to drag on for hours, when it fact it lasted a fraction of that time according to the clock (see Theme on Time). The strength of James's desire for adventure makes the period of anticipation seem far longer than it possibly can have been in chronometric terms. Is the reality of time the clock-face, or the lived experience?

A more general distinction is being made, between intensely personal subjective states and the physical reality of the objective world that is shared with others. This distinction pervades the novel. It is evident in the projection of James's inner bliss on to the picture of a refrigerator. Of crucial importance to Virginia Woolf was the fact that subjective and objective worlds interact. The external physical world enters into every individual's consciousness. Awareness of things outside the mind forms the content of that mind. That content is then coloured by the workings of an individual sensibility. So, a mundane item such as a picture of a refrigerator becomes, for a while, the focus for James's awareness. Simultaneously, that refrigerator, as it exists in the little boy's consciousness, is imbued with the joy which, at that moment, dominates his feelings about being alive (see Theme on Subject and Object and the Nature of Reality).

Mr Ramsay is obsessed with facts, while Mrs Ramsay is sensitive to feelings. This conforms to a standard division along gender lines in Virginia Woolf's work (see Theme on Gender). Men conventionally belong to the objective world of practical collective action. Women conventionally belong to the intimate, private world of personal sensations and emotions. This distinction is central to her characterisation. It is also an important component of the social criticism offered by this novel (see Theme on Social Criticism).

James is cutting pictures from the catalogue of the Army and Navy Stores. This is an indirect evocation of the armed forces, which had endured the horrors of the First World War (1914–18) a decade before *To the Lighthouse* was published. The opening of the novel is set shortly before that war, which later intrudes brutally into the life of the Ramsay family. Here the reference serves to remind us that James will grow up to participate in a social world run according to conventionally masculine values. Those values promote philosophical analysis and scientific investigation, the professional interests of Mr Ramsay and William Bankes. But those masculine values also presided over conduct of the war, with its huge cost to human lives (see Theme on Social Criticism).

Mrs Ramsay imagines James as a judge or some other important public figure. It seems a huge imaginative leap from this small boy at play, but the act of cutting out can be seen as part of his masculine training. It stands **metonymically** for his entry into the masculine world. Separating and isolating are processes identified in this book with the analytical mind, which is conventionally masculine. Analysis is characteristic of Mr Ramsay's way of thinking and of looking at things. In contrast, Virginia Woolf attributes to women a capacity for synthesis, for bringing things together and making them whole. So we see Mrs Ramsay busily knitting throughout, and Lily Briscoe searching for the vital brush-stroke that will hold the elements of her picture together (see Theme on Gender).

James is using scissors. Later he cuts out a picture of a pocket knife with six blades (p. 15). Mr Ramsay, when he first appears, is said to be 'lean as a knife' (p. 4). Cutting objects are **symbols** of masculine values in the novel. They carry associations of mental acuity and of danger. On the other hand, the knitting needles that Mrs Ramsay wields, and Lily Briscoe's paintbrush are symbols of bonding and unification.

The objects featured in the Army and Navy Stores catalogue belong to a domestic world that seems remote from the public arena in which the war was conducted; actually though, they belong to the fabric of the same patriarchal society. Virginia Woolf sustains a tension, however, between public and private, home and outside world. Following the fashion of middle-class Victorian England, in which her own parents had grown up, she identifies the domestic sphere with women and conventionally feminine values, and the public world with men and conventionally masculine values. Virginia Woolf is schematic in the way she sustains this division, but her intention is ultimately critical of its authority (see Theme on Gender).

Note Virginia Woolf's use of parenthesis, '(James thought)' (p. 4). She relies upon a fluent narrative voice, which resists attempts to impose upon it a neat, readily grasped identity. The voice is capable of passing from one individual's consciousness to another. Parenthetical phrases such as this allow her to attribute words to a particular person, without breaking the flow of her prose. That flow reflects the fact that the rest of the world does not pause while a character formulates a thought, or makes a statement, but continues in all its complex multiplicity. We may choose to see a significant parallel between Virginia Woolf's unifying narrative technique and Mrs Ramsay's dedication to drawing people together.

Mrs Ramsay's knitting acts as a symbol of her desire for wholeness. It also indicates her care for other people. She is making a gift for the son of the lighthouse-keeper, who is unwell. Her compassion contrasts with her husband's apparent self-centredness. She shows concern for the potentially dangerous situation of a one-armed man, pasting a poster to a wall. Indeed, she has taken sufficient interest to know that the man lost his arm through an accident with a reaping machine (p. 10). She has a capacity to imagine what it must be like to be someone else, someone very different from herself. This, Virginia Woolf would have recognised, is a necessary capacity for anyone practising the novelist's art.

The reaping machine is a further example of a cutting object associated with the activities of men. Here the capacity of such objects to mutilate is emphasised.

The time scheme of this section is complex. A brief exchange of a few words is extended by exploration of the processes of consciousness of those engaged in the dialogue. The dialogue itself would actually take place very quickly. The narration slows it down through disclosure of complex interior responses. It is as if, when reading it, we are experiencing the dialogue in slow motion. Virginia Woolf is injecting awareness of subjective states into her report of objectively simple utterances. In this way we are again alerted to the disparity between time as lived and time as measured.

There is also an extended **flashback** sequence, in which Mrs Ramsay's walk to town accompanied by Charles Tansley is recalled in some detail. The characters of both are elaborated in the process. More significantly, the technique shows how memory of past events forms an important part of our awareness in the present. In fact, the present continually modulates between anticipation of future events and recollection of what has already occurred. Often we have little or no control over the way in which memories spring into consciousness. Virginia Woolf, like her French contemporary Marcel Proust (1871–1922), was fascinated by involuntary recollection, where a trivial event or insignificant object triggers remembrance (see Theme on Time).

Charles Tansley has studied to advance himself socially, overcoming the material disadvantages of his working-class upbringing. His discomfort at Mrs Ramsay's proposal that they visit a circus shows his sensitivity to any suggestion, even when unintended, that he lacks refinement. He readily interprets Mr Carmichael's apparent withdrawal from meaningful social interaction as evidence that men should take wives who are willing to subject themselves to their husbands' careers. Mrs Ramsay is such a wife; so was Virginia Woolf's own mother, but the novelist reacted against this orthodoxy (see Theme on Gender). Alert to the challenge posed by class distinctions, Tansley remains tellingly indifferent to oppression of women.

Ibsen Henrik Ibsen (1828–1906), eminent but controversial Norwegian dramatist

the blue ribbon of the Garter order of knighthood, established in 1348 by Edward III, conventionally regarded as the highest form of British civil and military honour

2

Charles Tansley reiterates that there will be no trip to the Lighthouse the following day. He tries to seem genial, but nonetheless Mrs Ramsay considers him odious.

> This is a very brief section, which returns us to the here and now after the lengthy **flashback** that concluded the preceding section. The irregular length of sections throughout the book constitutes a distinctive structural rhythm. Virginia Woolf is not regulating her narrative divisions mechanically, like clockwork. Rather, she seems to be mirroring the irregularity of our experience of lived events. Some sections are extended; some are extremely compact. Her form is elastic and flexible, as it must be to accommodate her fluent narrative and complex characterisation.
>
> Mrs Ramsay's response to Tansley can be compared to James's response to his father. The boy's reaction is obviously more extreme, but he and his mother both perceive a tyrannical element in the attitudes of the two men. At times, in the course of the novel, Mrs Ramsay feels very differently about Tansley. It is an important part of Virginia Woolf's approach to characterisation that human responses are seen to be various to the point of inconsistency (see Characterisation).

3

Mrs Ramsay seeks to comfort James, and to distract him by finding a picture in the catalogue which will prove difficult to cut out. The voices of the men outside fall silent. She becomes aware of the sound of the waves on the shore. Then she hears her husband reciting lines from 'The Charge of the Light Brigade', a poem by Alfred, Lord Tennyson. It is his habit to do so, but Mrs Ramsay is still a little embarrassed by this eccentricity.

She sees Lily Briscoe, standing on the edge of the lawn, painting. Mrs Ramsay is part of the picture, and has been asked to sit as still as possible.

Although Mrs Ramsay seeks to comfort James, to compensate with kindness for the brutal frankness of the men, she does not respond in other than a protective way. There is no attempt to challenge directly conventionally masculine behaviour, nor to preclude the likelihood that James will one day emulate his father's ways. She is a caring but essentially conservative figure, much closer in character to Julia Stephen than to her daughter, Virginia Woolf.

Waves are a recurring motif in Virginia Woolf's writing. Indeed, she entitled her most ambitious novel, *The Waves* (1931). Here, in *To the Lighthouse*, they introduce an insistent natural rhythm, unaffected by human concerns. But waves carried greater symbolic weight for Virginia Woolf. The force which drives them is constant, a continuous rolling energy, but individual waves are themselves evanescent. They appear on the sea's surface, but quickly disperse, and may be seen to symbolise the way events form and dissolve within life's continuum. More poignantly, waves can be seen as symbols of individual human lives; each is a manifestation of something more fundamental, the condition of being alive. Each life is transient, destined to break and disappear. Human beings must at some point confront their own mortality, knowing that life will go on after their demise as it did before their birth.

It is characteristic of Mrs Ramsay that she seeks to interpret the sound of the breaking waves as an affirmation of protection and support, of the kind she offers to her own children. But she cannot conceal from herself an alternative interpretation, acknowledging the destructive passage of time that is beaten out by the sea's recurrent pulsing.

Another insistent sound enters dramatically into this section: Mr Ramsay's recitation of verse by the Victorian Poet Laureate, Alfred, Lord Tennyson (1809–92). His behaviour appears a harmless eccentricity, but this poem commemorates a battle of the Crimean War, and raises the spectre of human death in combat. *To the Lighthouse* was written in the long shadow cast by the First World War, with its unprecedentedly massive loss of life. Mr Ramsay's fondness for the poem discloses his affinity with a sense of military heroism, which the brutal realities of the First World War were soon to render obsolete. The action of this first part of the novel precedes that traumatic war, which occurred in the course of the second part, 'Time Passes'.

Lily, painting at the edge of the lawn provides a textual echo of the painter at the sea's edge, recalled by Mrs Ramsay in I, 1. Such echoes, together with the recurrence of **motifs**, help to bind Virginia Woolf's prose into coherence in the absence of a strong **story**

4

Mr Ramsay, waving his hands and reciting loudly, nearly collides with Lily Briscoe's easel. Then, Lily is aware of William Bankes approaching. He stands beside her. When Ramsay reappears, still declaiming Tennyson, Bankes suggests that Lily should take a stroll with him. In part he seeks to defuse embarrassment arising from their host's eccentric behaviour, but also it has become a regular walk for them, through the garden, to watch the waves in the bay.

The distant sand hills make Bankes think of Mr Ramsay, who enjoys that view. He recalls an occasion when Ramsay spoke, with uncharacteristic and almost sentimental warmth, of a hen that spread her wings to protect her chicks. Bankes notices Cam, the youngest Ramsay daughter, picking flowers, accompanied by her nursemaid. He is musing on the cost of raising a family of eight children, for the Ramsays although comfortably off are not rich, when Jasper Ramsay approaches and, shaking Lily's hand, declares he has just shot at a bird. Bankes discusses with Lily Briscoe the pros and cons of having a family. Mr Ramsay's philosophical work becomes the focus of their conversation. Bankes feels that Mr Ramsay has been diminished, as a thinker and as a man, because he has family obligations.

Lily muses on how people come to feel they have knowledge of one another. She is drawn back to the external world by a shot fired by Jasper. A flock of starlings takes to the air. The couple pass through a gap in the hedge and encounter Mr Ramsay, seemingly in a world of his own, still reciting the poem. He appears resentful of their intrusion, and turns away from them. The starlings settle on the tops of elm trees.

An important aspect of this novel is Virginia Woolf's investigation of the nature of relationships between men and women, of the details and nuances that can form a bond between ostensibly very different people. The Ramsays provide the primary example, but another is offered in this section: William Bankes is a scientist; Lily Briscoe is an artist. She views plants aesthetically; he dissects and classifies them. The two characters see the world from different angles, each aligned to conventional gender stereotypes, yet there are points of convergence, and a form of mutual attraction becomes evident.

Bankes's recollection of Ramsay's comments about the hen constitutes a structural parallel to Mrs Ramsay's **flashback** to her walk with Tansley, in I, 1. Both illustrate the role of memory in our sense of the present. There is also a thematic parallel between the hen anecdote and the protectiveness shown towards James by Mrs Ramsay. Mr Ramsay feels that a maternal instinct is natural to the female of the species, and Mrs Ramsay concurs. But Lily, a woman of a younger generation, and an artist, does not manifest maternal instincts. Comparably, while her mother had seven children, Virginia Woolf remained childless.

It was after seeing the hen that Ramsay married and began his family. Was such an apparently incidental event the cause from which his marriage followed as effect?

In Bankes's view, work and family make contesting demands, and, however focused in study Ramsay may appear to be, his friend suspects that the responsibilities of fatherhood have drained energies which might otherwise have served philosophy. In discussing Ramsay's achievement, Bankes observes that 'the number of men who make a definite contribution to anything whatsoever is very small' (p. 22). Note the gendered nature of this observation. Few men make a worthwhile addition to the world's knowledge, but women it seems do not even merit mention. As a feminist Virginia Woolf spoke out against such exclusion (see Theme on Gender).

Virginia Woolf writes of impressions that pour in upon Lily. The novelist was acutely aware that human beings are bombarded constantly by sensory data, yet somehow we manage to filter order from it all. Language helps us to map a stable reality amidst the myriad impressions of the day, but Virginia Woolf recognised that naive identification of words with the volatile non-verbal world is reductive. Reality is too fleeting and multifaceted to be encapsulated through simple description. As a mature writer she strove to establish a more accurate means to represent the relationship between language and experience than could be found in conventional **realist fiction** or in the accounts offered by scientists and philosophers.

'Subject and object and the nature of reality' is Andrew Ramsay's summary of the field covered by his father's work in philosophy. To clarify this for Lily's understanding, he suggests 'Think of a kitchen table then ... when you're not there' (p. 21). The relationship between a perceiving consciousness and the object of its perception has generated a great deal of philosophical thought. It was one of the issues that occupied George Edward Moore (1873–1958), a philosopher associated with the Bloomsbury Group to which Virginia Woolf also belonged (see Literary Background – The Bloomsbury Group).

Lily cannot cope with the abstractions of philosophical discourse, and clings to the homely image of that table in order to sustain some connection with Mr Ramsay's work. Similarly, thinking of William Bankes's work in the laboratory she involuntarily visualises 'sections of potatoes' used in experiments (p. 22). Virginia Woolf preserves a conventional gender distinction, which associates a capacity for abstract thought with the masculine mind, while feminine thought processes are imbedded in physical reality. Philosophy and science are consequently regarded as male domains.

We should, however, recognise that as an artist Lily is involved with exactly those issues that obsess Mr Ramsay. Her work, representing the objective world as it is filtered through her own subjective awareness, constitutes a serious aesthetic statement concerning 'subject and object and the nature of reality'. A comparable aesthetic statement was achieved by Virginia Woolf in her fiction. Neither Lily Briscoe nor Virginia Woolf found the language of philosophy, or that of science, congenial to their purpose, but for both art has a capacity to render truth.

Virginia Woolf is being **ironic** when she writes that reduction of reality to 'angular essences' is the mark of the finest minds. According to that definition, the finest minds would be exclusively philosophical and masculine. She recognised that appreciation of 'lovely evenings, with all their flamingo clouds and blue and silver' is equally a quality of a fine mind, although it is one assigned conventionally to a feminine sensibility, and so devalued in a patriarchal society (p. 21). That irony, deprecating modern European culture's elevation of the value of abstraction above that of physical reality, recurs in the characterisation of Mr Ramsay that follows in the next section.

Lily Briscoe experiences two particular sensations while talking with William Bankes: in one, all she herself feels subjectively about him is concentrated; in the other, she apprehends the objective existence of the man himself. In effect, she is, through intuition, grasping basic propositions formulated in Mr Ramsay's philosophy. Virginia Woolf's schematic division along gender lines has men better equipped to think rationally about the nature of the world; but women exist more fully in the lived world of moment-to-moment experience.

The way Lily regards Bankes, in his isolation and impersonality, may be compared to the way James, as a child, looks at the Lighthouse. Both are looming presences in the observer's consciousness, yet both have their own self-contained existence. Lily is prompted to ask herself how liking for another person is formed and recognised:

How did one judge people, think of them? How did one add up this and that and conclude that it was liking one felt, or disliking? And to those words, what meaning attached, after all? (p. 22)

Virginia Woolf is investigating how links between subjective beings are established, how we come to experience fellow-feeling.

Language works as a system of conventional and general meanings; it seems a blunt instrument with which to fathom subtle interactions between discrete and distinctive human beings. But language forms a bridge between the individual consciousness and the collective understanding of a social group. The words each of us uses to think are not personal property, but are collectively owned. So, the nature of language itself appears to narrow the gap between subject and object; the words available to each of us to talk of the self come from the outside. The language is there before an individual's birth, and remains after an individual's death. Virginia Woolf recognised that the serious novelist, a virtuoso with words, is especially well placed to address aesthetically questions of 'subject and object and the nature of reality'.

Balaclava battle fought in 1854, during the Crimean War. The Charge of the Light Brigade, which Tennyson later commemorated in his poem, occurred in the course of this battle

Westmorland former county in north-west England, now part of Cumbria

5

Mrs Ramsay assures James that if the weather is unsuitable tomorrow, there will, in the near future, be another fine day. She watches Lily Briscoe with William Bankes, and feels they should marry.

James is resentful that his mother uses his leg to measure a stocking she is making for the lighthouse-keeper's son. Mrs Ramsay notes the shabbiness of the chairs, left throughout the winter in a house susceptible to damp. But the place is cheap and spacious, the children love it, and it allows her husband to relax, three hundred miles from his library and his lecturing obligations. Nonetheless, she is unsettled by the state of the house, and its gradual decrepitude.

She recalls an occasion when Bankes telephoned her, and commented on her beauty. In the present, Mrs Ramsay continues to knit, and kisses James before helping him find another picture to cut out.

Remember that this part of the novel is called 'The Window'. Mrs Ramsay observes events in the garden from the drawing-room window, through which her husband and Charles Tansley have added their unwelcome contributions. Here she notes that doors in the house are invariably open; her rule, on the other hand, is 'that windows should be open, and doors shut' (p. 25). This may be read in **figurative** terms, suggesting that individuals should preserve their privacy, yet remain receptive to experience, keeping their senses alert.

Mrs Ramsay's openness to experience is compromised by her commitment to domestic obligations. She is dedicated to the role allocated to her as an upper-middle-class wife and mother, the role of being 'Mrs Ramsay'. Her husband is steeped in the culture of books, and he habitually recites poetry. But she has no time, or perhaps inclination, even to read books given to her in person by a poet. In I, 19 we do see Mrs Ramsay reading, but her activity is undertaken primarily to create a bond with her husband.

The shabbiness of the house, worsening yearly, introduces a melancholic sense of time passing, which will come to the fore in the novel's middle part, 'Time Passes'. The mood is intensified here when Mrs Ramsay thinks sympathetically of the Swiss girl they employ, whose father is dying in distant mountains. The Ramsays employ several servants; although not rich, according to William Bankes, they are evidently far from poor.

James's resentment at being used as a measure for the stocking discloses selfishness, which contrasts with his mother's compassionate care for others. There is a suggestion here, however, that he has inherited from her that tendency to exaggerate evident in the novel's opening pages. She muses that 'it did her husband good to be three thousand, or if she must be accurate, three hundred miles from his library and his lectures and his disciples' (p. 25). This tendency is indicative of an imaginative nature, which in James's case will become increasingly suppressed as he grows towards conventional manhood.

The Graces Greek goddesses of fertility
Euston railway station in central London
Michael Angelo Michelangelo di Lodovico Buonarroti (1475–1564), Italian artist, sculptor and poet

6

Mrs Ramsay's musing is interrupted by the sound of her husband's recitation. She sees that he is disturbed by the unexpected encounter with Lily Briscoe and William Bankes. She strokes James's head. Her husband regains his composure.

Pausing at the window, Mr Ramsay uses a sprig to tickle his son's leg. James is resentful, but his father persists in teasing him. Husband and wife continue to disagree over the prospects for tomorrow's planned voyage.

Mr Ramsay retreats into the garden, initially reciting, then humming and eventually falling silent. The narrative voice considers the nature of Mr Ramsay's 'splendid mind' (p. 31). His strengths, but also his limitations and his fear of failure are made clear. He conceives his work as a heroic enterprise; it has earned him the right to pay homage to the beauty he sees in his wife and son.

> The workings of Mr Ramsay's mind are described as linear, like keys on a piano, or letters of the alphabet. In those terms his mind seems 'splendid', but Virginia Woolf understood reality as a field of experience, with many and various things happening at the same time. It is possible to trace lines of reasoning across that field, but no single line is an adequate reflection of the complexity of existence. (For more detailed commentary upon the characterisation of Mr Ramsay found in this section, see Textual Analysis – Text 1.)

> For Mrs Ramsay, her husband's devotion to fact, irrespective of people's feelings, rends 'the thin veils of civilisation' (p. 29). For Virginia Woolf, as for many of her contemporaries in the arts, 'civilisation' was a precarious structure built by human beings over an abyss of meaninglessness (see Historical Background – Contemporary Pessimism). Preservation of civilisation required observance of certain rules. If those rules were violated, the whole structure could collapse. Mr Ramsay's lack of considerateness seems to his wife to constitute such a violation. Virginia Woolf saw the First World War as a much larger tear in the fabric of civilised existence. Its brutality forced a harrowing glimpse into the abyss. In

its wake, she enquired in her fiction into the prerequisites for a more compassionate structure of civilisation (see Theme on Social Criticism).

'There was nothing to be said' is a statement that encapsulates Mrs Ramsay's response to her husband's boorish behaviour (p. 30). It occurred earlier in order to convey her response to the Swiss girl, sorrowing for her terminally ill father. Mr Ramsay prides himself on his erudition and articulateness, his precision in using language. But for his wife and, towards the end of the novel, for Lily Briscoe also, there are evident limits to the expressive capacity of language. The First World War created a widespread sense amongst writers that there were experiences of the human body so intense that they defied formulation in words. Virginia Woolf's writing strives to find more effective ways to convey the value of human existence and of individual being.

Mrs Ramsay often thinks of herself as 'a sponge sopped full of human emotions'. The children go to her all day long with various requests, 'naturally, since she was a woman' (p. 30). The word 'naturally' appears **ironic** here, as such responsibilities are assigned to women through social pressures, rather than through 'natural' necessity. But Mrs Ramsay, fully engaged with the role of wife and mother that has been allocated to her, is not aware of the irony.

Mr Ramsay endorses the view that women are constitutionally different from and socially inferior to men. Observing irrationality in his wife's behaviour, he makes an extrapolation to attribute that characteristic to all women. He is furious at her refusal to face the facts registered on the barometer and in the wind's direction. But it is her fulfilment of her culturally determined role as caring mother that produces this refusal, as she strives to console her child. She is as capable as her husband of reading the barometer accurately, but she has other priorities.

Mr Ramsay says 'Damn you' to his wife, irate that she is lying to James about the weather prospects (p. 30); she nonetheless feels reverence for him. The love in this marriage remains largely unspoken, behind superficial disputes and disagreements, and beyond the reach of words. But Mrs Ramsay's sentiment that 'She was not good enough to tie his shoe strings' (p. 30) takes matters a step further. Virginia Woolf would doubtless have felt that such overt subservience was far too passive, too readily accepting of received definitions of social worth. Her feminism was a reaction against such patriarchal definitions.

7

James, with the heightened intensity of a child's temperament, hates his father, who refuses to leave him alone with his mother. At last, Mr Ramsay departs to watch the other children play cricket, leaving his wife to read a fairy story to their youngest son. Mr Carmichael shuffles past, and Mrs Ramsay pauses to speak to him.

Mr Ramsay, who prizes the solitude required for his work, nonetheless requires sympathetic attention from his wife. These demands for sympathy betray an underlying lack of confidence. In the previous section, he admitted to himself that he was not a genius, yet Ramsay still looks to his wife for some confirmation of his worth. She cites Tansley's admiration for him, but he wants more: to be drawn out of his isolation and restored to 'the heart of life' (p. 35). The narrative voice presents his evident dependency as indication of 'the fatal sterility of the male', contrasted adversely with the 'delicious fecundity' of the female, 'this fountain and spray of life' (p. 34). Ramsay is like a child returning to its nurturing mother 'to have his senses restored to him, his barrenness made fertile' (p. 35). Virginia Woolf argued in the essay *Three Guineas* (1938) that the underlying immaturity of men caused much of the conflict in the world.

Blade imagery recurs with 'the arid scimitar of the male'. Mrs Ramsay, on the other hand, is compared to 'a rosy-flowered fruit tree' (p. 35). Although Virginia Woolf remained sceptical about the claims made by Sigmund Freud (1856–1939) for his practice of psychoanalysis, this section, with its focus upon tense familial relationships, and its deployment of **symbolic** language, offers rich ground for Freudian analysis (see Contemporary Approaches – Freudian Criticism).

Mrs Ramsay feels drained following her efforts to counteract her husband's insecurity. She also feels unsettled by the sound of the waves which reminds her of passing time, and so of her own mortality. She suddenly feels 'the inadequacy of human relationships', recognising 'that the most perfect was flawed' (p. 37). Characteristically, however, she feels compelled to speak to Mr Carmichael, seeking to connect with that isolated man.

8

Mr Carmichael, allegedly an opium addict, does not respond to Mrs Ramsay's words. She feels that he does not trust her, and she blames his wife for this. She returns to the story she is reading to James. But she is distracted by the presence of her husband, who has not, as he said he would, gone to watch the other children playing cricket.

Mr Ramsay is musing on Shakespeare, and, more generally, on human progress. Such issues will form a lecture he is to give in Cardiff in six weeks time.

The focus shifts to Lily Briscoe and William Bankes, who note the self-deprecation which reveals Mr Ramsay's sense that he is a failure professionally. They wonder 'why so brave a man in thought should be so timid in life' (p. 42). Lily comments upon the disparity between the world of thought Ramsay inhabits and the trivial concerns that engage those around him.

> Opium, it is suggested, serves to insulate Augustus Carmichael against human contact. He has retreated from active participation in relationships, and this distresses Mrs Ramsay, who devotes her energies to establishing and maintaining such connections between people. She is unsettled by his apparent lack of trust towards her, and lays the blame with his wife, who once turned him out of their house in St John's Wood, London, so the two women could be left alone to talk. Mrs Ramsay had, with characteristic intuition, sensed his misery.

Aware that her own kindnesses might seem to others to be acts of vanity, Mrs Ramsay dwells on the pettiness of human relations, 'how flawed they are, how despicable, how self-seeking, at their best' (p. 39). Her evident pessimism at such moments gives substance to her husband's later observation that she is a deeply pessimistic woman, despite the affirmative role she consistently plays in the life of the Ramsay family and their acquaintances.

Virginia Woolf's father spent many years editing the *Dictionary of National Biography*. This onerous task meant that he daily engaged with summaries of the careers of noteworthy historical figures. Perhaps recollection of that vast project lies behind Virginia Woolf's portrayal of Mr Ramsay, contemplating the relationship between the lives of great men and the progress of human civilisation.

Virginia Woolf felt that the predominance in historical accounts of men and conventional masculine values had been taken for granted for too long. It needed to be called into question as a matter of urgency following the First World War, in which the sagacity of men and the sanctity of their values had been graphically undermined by appalling suffering and death (see Theme on Social Criticism).

In the course of Ramsay's evaluation of the representativeness of 'the lot of the average human being' in gauging civilised values, he rejects the arts as an essential component of civilised society. He concludes that they are 'merely a decoration imposed on the top of human life; they do not express it' (p. 40). Virginia Woolf would have disagreed fundamentally with this estimation; for her the arts were the vital expression of human life and the most reliable index of civilised values. We have recently witnessed Mrs Ramsay lamenting her husband's violation of those values. It is **ironic** that he now assumes professional expertise on the topic of civilisation.

Virginia Woolf uses an extended **simile** to describe in terms of a man on horseback the course taken by Ramsay's thoughts (p. 40). They now follow a well-trodden path, as Bankes has already remarked. Ramsay is not an original thinker, and there comes a point where he is forced to dismount, (before the letter R in terms of the simile elaborated in section I, 6).

Mr Ramsay is next compared to a 'desolate sea-bird', isolated on a spit of land that is being steadily eroded (p. 41). Virginia Woolf uses **figurative language** to evoke the fate of this man, stranded at a particularly bleak moment in intellectual history (see Historical Background – Contemporary Pessimism). In this way, she helps us to understand why Bankes, Tansley, and Mrs Ramsay all admire this tetchy and eccentric man. His intensity and determination, amidst erosive uncertainties, command allegiance. Yet it is **ironic** that Virginia Woolf should employ blatantly literary devices to convey the intellectual heroism of this man, who has just denied the enduring value of art. By doing so, she is undermining the validity of his views, while simultaneously indicating that he is nonetheless a man worthy of respect.

the Tube   the underground railway in London
Locke   John Locke (1632–1704), English philosopher, and author of *Essay Concerning Human Understanding* (1690)
Hume   David Hume (1711–76), Scottish philosopher and historian, and author of *Treatise of Human Nature* (1740)
Berkeley   George Berkeley (1685–1753), Irish philosopher, who wrote about the relationship between perceiver and perceived

9

Bankes laments Mr Ramsay's unusual behaviour, which he feels distances him from other people. Lily Briscoe dislikes Ramsay's 'narrowness, his blindness' (p. 43).

Lily contemplates her picture with dissatisfaction, and is critical in her thoughts of Mrs Ramsay, whom she feels has been high-handed recently.

Bankes examines Lily's picture. They discuss it, and she feels they are drawn together into a form of intimacy. Cam Ramsay dashes past.

Virginia Woolf has Lily Briscoe use one of her own favourite images, a wave, to cast light on the unificatory influence of love in the world:

life, from being made up of little separate incidents which one lived one by one, became curled and whole like a wave which bore one up with it and threw one down with it, there, with a dash on the beach (p. 44)

In this image, the complex of emotions identified by that simple word 'love' seems to enable human beings to experience a sense of life's wholeness. It also appears hazardous, invariably involving that potentially damaging 'dash on the beach'.

Seeing Mrs Ramsay reading to her son, Bankes is affected by this manifestation of maternal love in precisely the same way as when 'he had proved something absolute about the digestive system of plants', feeling that 'barbarity was tamed, the reign of chaos subdued' (p. 44). He recognises an affirmation of order.

Mrs Ramsay strives throughout to act as an ordering centre, granting coherence to the lives of the group. For Virginia Woolf, writing was a comparable affirmation of order in a chaotic world. The work of literary art draws the fragments of reality into meaningful form. Lily's dedication to painting is similarly an effort to create an enclave of meaning, which may also serve as a bridge between the self and the world beyond the self (see Theme on Art). Lily recalls how Charles Tansley goaded her with his patriarchal prejudice that 'Women can't paint, women can't write …' (p. 45). As a feminist, Virginia Woolf sought to counter such exclusion of women from assessments of cultural achievement.

Yet Lily is critical of her own work; she feels it is inadequate. Like Virginia Woolf, she wishes to convey the stable structure of being, underlying the evanescent surface of experience: 'She saw the colour burning on a framework of steel; the light of a butterfly's wing lying upon the arches of a cathedral' (p. 45). Being, which embraces all forms of life, is always present. It is the life of the world, as it has been and as it will be, pulsing away under the surface of the most trivial occurrences within the course of an individual's life. We enter into being when we are born, but it does not cease with any individual's death. This is the crucial point made in the second part of the novel, 'Time Passes', where death touches the Ramsay family, and the life of the world continues regardless.

Lily ponders an issue of crucial concern to Virginia Woolf, as a novelist engaged in characterisation: 'How then, she had asked herself, did one know one thing or another thing about people, sealed as they were?' (p. 48). Imaginatively, Lily conceives of herself as a bee, visiting the hive that is Mrs Ramsay. Prior to that she considers the need for a 'device for becoming, like waters poured into one jar, inextricably the same, one with the object one adored' (p. 47). The novel returns to its concern with overcoming the distance between subject and object; 'love' is a convenient term to identify this bridge. But Lily desires total identification, 'nothing that could be written in any language known to men, but intimacy itself, which is knowledge' (p. 47). Clearly, it is not knowledge as Mr Ramsay would recognise it.

A recurrent concern of *To the Lighthouse* is the inexpressibility of some of the most important truths of human existence. Words cannot adequately convey certain states and relationships. Virginia Woolf again uses **figurative language** to **ironic** effect, employing a highly wrought sentence, referring to sacred inscriptions, to highlight what cannot be said:

she imagined how in the chambers of the mind and heart of the woman who was, physically, touching her, were stood, like the treasures in the tombs of kings, tablets bearing sacred inscriptions, which if one could spell them out would teach one everything, but they would never be offered openly, never made public' (p. 47)

Compare this sense of hidden treasures to Mr Ramsay's faith in the power of language to express all that is of value.

Bankes taps Lily's picture with a penknife; the cutting edge of masculine analysis is suggested. The **symbolic** forms on the canvas do not conform to his scientific understanding. But he is interested in the assumptions underlying her approach to art. Through that interest an understanding forms, so that Lily feels 'This man had shared with her something profoundly intimate' (p. 50).

Carlyle   Thomas Carlyle (1795–1881), eminent Scottish Victorian thinker and writer

treasures in the tombs of kings Virginia Woolf perhaps had in mind the tomb of the ancient Egyptian king Tutankhamun, discovered in 1922 by Howard Carter

10

Cam dashes past, heeding neither Bankes, nor her father. Her mother calls out, and as Cam stands before her, preoccupied with her own imaginative concerns, Mrs Ramsay gives her an errand, to ask a question of Mildred the cook. Soon, Cam returns with the reply that her brother Andrew, Minta Doyle, and Paul Rayley have not yet returned.

Mrs Ramsay's mind dwells on Minta and Paul. Although she continues reading to James, she is thinking about the courtship and possible marriage of the two young visitors. She had earlier encouraged them to walk on the beach together, asserting that it would not rain. Cam departs.

Mrs Ramsay thinks about her children, their characters and their future. She continues to read to James. It is dusk, and she grows increasingly anxious about Andrew and the others, still not returned from their coastal walk. She envisages accidents, but she continues reading.

As the story reaches its conclusion, she notices her son's attention turning to the rays emanating from the Lighthouse. She anticipates his question, and also her reply, but Mildred arrives to carry James off to bed.

> Despite appearances, Mrs Ramsay considers her husband to be happier, more positive, more free from care than herself. The crucial difference appears to be that he can lose himself in study, and avoid the kind of introspection to which she is prone. The impersonal nature of his work preserves him from the inward-looking tendency that breeds anxiety in his sensitive, caring wife. Her days are spent protecting her family from potential dangers, and she has a heightened sense of what troubles may befall human beings. Her fear is that she and life are in some way opposed; it is 'terrible, hostile, and quick to pounce on you if you gave it a chance'. She cites as eternal problems, 'suffering; death; the poor' (p. 55).

> Mrs Ramsay's affirmative sense of marriage and parenthood is cast in another light by her admission that 'she was driven on, too

quickly she knew, almost as if it were an escape for her too, to say that people must marry; people must have children' (p. 56). She seeks principles of order in a world inclined to chaos. The contract of marriage **symbolises** the union of two separate beings in a relationship of trust and mutuality. It counters, symbolically and sometimes in practical terms, the isolation and fragmentedness that Mrs Ramsay abhors. Parenthood can be seen as a symbolic compensation for the mother and father's mortality. Their own death is inevitable, but the birth of their children is affirmation of being. There is, then, a kind of desperation underlying Mrs Ramsay's seemingly benign desire to see couples wed and families started.

11

Left alone, Mrs Ramsay now feels she can be herself. She attains a level of being, unreachable amid the distractions of the day, allowing her increased imaginative freedom. She feels at one with the Lighthouse, whose beam flashes out with hypnotic rhythm.

Mr Ramsay, passing by, notices a sternness at the heart of his wife's beauty. He feels suddenly incapable of helping her in her isolated sadness.

Fixing her attention on the Lighthouse beam, Mrs Ramsay feels a connection to the world, and is aware of the intense happiness she has known. The beauty of the scene, as the light plays across the water, is enough to justify living.

Simultaneously, Mr Ramsay sees his wife's loveliness. He feels unable to interrupt her solitude, but she takes her shawl and goes to him, recognising his desire to offer her protection.

For a more detailed commentary on this section see Textual Analysis – Text 2.

The elucidation of Mrs Ramsay's character, which we encountered in the previous section, is continued here. Mrs Ramsay experiences a sense of freedom arising as she contemplates the Lighthouse rays; at the same time she is conscious of human mortality, and aware that her own life will come to an end. She is cross with herself for momentarily lapsing into a platitudinous belief in the Lord, a patriarchal God in whom she really has no faith. She feels that 'there is no reason, order, justice: but suffering, death, the poor' (p. 59), an echo from page 55.

Mr Ramsay's life's work is focused in reason, order, and justice, although his personal behaviour often appears unreasonable, disordered and unjust. Mrs Ramsay's bleak vision, usually concealed by her efforts to alleviate the discomfort and unease of others, is characteristic of a pessimism that had taken hold in the late-Victorian period, and was insistently felt in the writings of the generation to which Virginia Woolf belonged. It followed from widespread loss of faith in orthodox religion, and erosion of belief in the notion that social progress was inevitable (see Historical Background – Contemporary Pessimism).

Forms of mutual affection and appreciation between the Ramsays are clearly signalled in this section. The word 'love' might be applied to what they experience, but words are not really a part of the experience. Bridges are formed primarily through non-verbal communication between them.

12

It is just past seven o'clock in the evening. Mrs Ramsay walks with her husband in the garden. They discuss Charles Tansley, Kennedy the gardener, and their children. Mr Ramsay comments on his wife's earlier sadness. They become uncomfortable with one another, and he declares his intention to go off for a walk, alone, tomorrow, if the weather holds. She knows he will not do so.

As they talk they seem to grow apart, then Mr Ramsay kisses his wife's hand with an intensity that draws them together again. They walk arm in arm around the garden, together, yet occupying their separate worlds.

Mrs Ramsay catches sight of Bankes and Lily walking together, and her mind springs to the possibility of their marrying.

Following the emphasis upon non-verbal communication in the preceding section, we here encounter in abundance the phrases 'said Mr Ramsay' and 'said Mrs Ramsay', signalling relatively straightforward dialogue. However, the verbal exchange does not convey the emotional commitment between the couple, which cannot be readily formulated in words. Conversation resembles the breaking of waves on the surface, while far more significant non-verbal communication occurs unceasingly below.

Mr Ramsay espouses the view that it is 'natural' for a boy to shoot. His argument is that it is not social conditioning, but a biological impulse that inclines men rather than women towards aggressive behaviour. Not long after this conversation, the First World War saw the deaths of millions of men. Political and economic factors, not biological determinants, governed the conduct of that terrible war. Mr Ramsay's view of masculine proclivities matches his oppressive sense of which social roles are 'natural' for women. Virginia Woolf accepted that gender characteristics were deeply engrained, but as a feminist she challenged the argument that they were unchanging (see Theme on Gender).

Mr Ramsay appears to share his wife's view that parenthood is a way to counter the threat of chaos. He feels that having eight children has been 'a good bit of work on the whole', and remarks that Andrew's professional success and Prue's beauty should 'stem the flood a bit' (p. 64).

Mrs Ramsay feels that her husband says many things merely for effect: 'All this phrase-making was a game' (p. 64). Conversations are presented throughout as a kind of game, with another level of meaning existing beyond the words. Ramsay kisses his wife's hand; this action brings tears to her eyes. But she wants him to share the pleasure of looking at the evening star, and she knows he will not really look at it. Mr Ramsay's conventionally masculine egotism prevents him entering into communion with the world beyond the self. His recitations of poetry are perhaps a form of defence against the intrusiveness he fears from conversation.

Mrs Ramsay can hold disparate thoughts in her mind simultaneously; she thinks of her husband's rarefied world of books and lecture halls while she tends the garden and considers practical measures to keep the rabbits out. Those rabbits, relatively innocuous when taken literally, may be seen as **symbols** of the chaos that Mrs Ramsay assiduously seeks to keep at bay.

Best and brightest, come away! from the poem 'To Jane: The Invitation' by Percy Bysshe Shelley (1792–1822)

13

Bankes talks of his European travels, and of the pictures he has seen. Lily speaks of her more limited experience of travel, and refers to the dissatisfaction she feels with her own work whenever she sees great art. Still, she will continue to paint because it interests her.

Mr and Mrs Ramsay watch their children Prue and Jasper throwing a ball to one another. The Ramsays become for Lily 'the symbols of marriage' (p. 67).

Lily Briscoe is a relatively independent woman, moving with greater freedom than most women of the preceding generation. She has been to Brussels, to Dresden, and to Paris to assist a sick aunt, but unlike Bankes she has not reached Rome, with its art treasures. In I, 11 Mrs Ramsay imagines herself at a church in Rome, and on the plains of India. Imagination is her means to overcome the constraints of physical circumstance, in order to reach 'all the places she had not seen' (p. 58). To regard men as adventurers, while women stay at home, is a cultural cliché dating back at least to the ancient Greek epic the *Odyssey*. In I, '6 Mr Ramsay's characteristic qualities are described as those required by the leader of a polar expedition (p. 32).

Lily Briscoe's dissatisfaction with her own work may be seen to parallel Mr Ramsay's sense of failure. Despite their obvious differences, and the wider spectrum of opportunity open to the man, they share a basic sense that more might be accomplished than they have managed. Perhaps Virginia Woolf is suggesting that although this is a common fate for all who seek to make a contribution to civilised life, men and women, the important thing is to make the effort, and to add something, rather than being content with what is already in place.

Virginia Woolf's technique of shifting perspective involves overlapping in time. In place of the single fixed point of view that has dominated conventional narratives, she boldly presents spatially differentiated points of view, existing simultaneously. So, in the preceding section Mrs Ramsay observed Lily and Bankes together; now Lily observes the Ramsays. These two perceptions presumably coincided, or were close together in time; the narration stretches that moment in order to shift from one position to the other.

The Ramsays exist in the physical world, and they exist as objects of Lily's consciousness. In Lily's mind, they briefly assume symbolic value. Just as the image of a kitchen table earlier stood in her mind for the abstractions that preoccupied the philosopher, so these familiar figures serve as 'symbols of marriage', granting physical reality to the concept (p. 67).

Obsessions indicate the separateness of characters, despite the scene's concern with the mutuality of marriage. Mr Ramsay returns to the image of the philosopher Hume, stuck in a bog, and feels able to laugh aloud at the image, although it exists only privately, within his mind. Mrs Ramsay, on the other hand, returns to worrying about the late return of Andrew, Nancy, Minta and Paul. She is anxious; her husband is laughing. Her anxiety springs from concern for others, while his laughter is self-contained.

Rembrandts paintings by the Dutch artist Rembrandt Harmensz van Rijn (1606–69)
Prado famous art gallery in Madrid
the Sistine Chapel chapel in the Vatican Palace containing famous frescoes by Michelangelo
Giotto Giotto di Bondone (1267–1337), an Italian painter and architect
Titian Tiziano Vecellio (d.1576) an Italian painter
Darwin Charles Darwin (1809–82), English naturalist who formulated an immensely influential theory of evolution

14

Nancy Ramsay was persuaded by Minta Doyle to join her, Paul Rayley and Andrew for a coastal walk. Andrew Ramsay is impressed by Minta's tomboyish character; she seems frightened of nothing except bulls. As the same time, he recognises foolhardiness in her behaviour.

Minta insists that the others join her in singing a popular song of the period. Nancy investigates a rock pool, which is transformed through the workings of her imagination. Then, she comes across Paul and Minta embracing. She is outraged by the spectacle.

Minta loses her grandmother's brooch, and cries. Paul, Andrew and Nancy have to search for it. Minta is suddenly fearful at the prospect of being cut off by the tide.

Paul has asked Minta to marry him; he is anxious as a consequence, and vows to ask Mrs Ramsay for advice, as it was her influence that made him propose.

Darkness is falling as they return to the house, which is lit up. There, preparations for dinner are in progress.

This section blurs the distinction between a **flashback**, tracing the departure of the group for the shore, and an account of action occurring simultaneously with the events we have witnessed at the Ramsay household.

Minta fears being cut off by the tide. Andrew observes that 'she had no control over her emotions' (p. 71). He adds, 'Women hadn't', disclosing a propensity, shared with his father, to derive a general principle from a specific instance, especially if it appears to confirm the inferiority of women. Andrew's impression of Minta's character is revised as her anxieties come to the surface. Virginia Woolf felt that neat formulations are never adequate to encapsulate human character. Minta's bold facade is actually a way of coping with deeply felt anxieties. Compare the way in which Mrs Ramsay is insistently affirmative in order to conceal profound fears.

The vision of Constantinople, used to give substance to Nancy's vague desires and aspirations, connects with the discussion of Rome in I, 13, and with Mrs Ramsay's imaginary flight to India and to Rome in I, 11. Figuring Nancy's desire for experience of the world, Constantinople occupies a position in her consciousness comparable to that which the Lighthouse occupies in James's mind.

The exotic location represents longing for unspecified freedoms, denied by the routine realities of home. For the moment at least, Nancy, like her mother, relies on the imagination to compensate for physical limits placed upon her.

The four young people display vestiges of childishness, although emerging into the world of adult responsibility. Paul, following his proposal of marriage to Minta feels 'It had been far and away the worst moment of his life' (p. 72). It is typical of Virginia Woolf's characterisation to depict a response in which happiness and misery are intertwined, or unexpectedly displace one another.

Constantinople Turkish city, now called Istanbul
Santa Sofia ancient Christian church, subsequently a mosque
the Golden Horn a channel of water running through Istanbul

15

A single sentence, which returns us to the question that preceded section 14. Prue responds to her mother's question, affirming that Nancy did go with the group.

The bold disparity in the length of sections establishes an idiosyncratic structural rhythm.

16

Mrs Ramsay is in her room, attending to her appearance, prior to dinner. Jasper and Rose enter with a message from Mildred, the cook. Mrs Ramsay is still anxious about the late return of Nancy, Andrew, Minta, and Paul, but her anxiety inclines towards annoyance. She discusses with her children the rooks that can be seen from the window.

Andrew and the others return. Mrs Ramsay feels annoyed with them, but is excited at the prospect of an engagement between Minta and Paul. She descends to the dining room, and the gong for dinner is sounded.

Mrs Ramsay's concern over the lateness of the group gives way to annoyance at their inconsiderateness. Virginia Woolf again shows the mixed nature of human responses. Mrs Ramsay's anxiety about her dinner party is enough to modify her feelings about the young people's absence, allowing irritation to surface.

The rooks form a recurring **motif**, helping to bind together a novel that does not tell a story in any conventional sense. This is the most extended discussion of the birds. Mrs Ramsay finds them amusing, and calls the two main rooks Joseph and Mary, perhaps an impious indication of her lack of Christian belief. The birds fight, and their wings are described as 'scimitar shapes' (p. 75), recalling the blade imagery used earlier in the novel in association with conventionally masculine attitudes.

The items of jewellery Mrs Ramsay has to choose between are from Italy and India, destinations for her imaginative journey in I, 11. She is especially attracted to these places because she has some Italian ancestry, while her uncle spent time in India.

In her instructions to Rose and Jasper with regard to proper social behaviour, Mrs Ramsay reinforces conventional gender stereotypes. She is deeply conservative in terms of the politics of gender.

Boeuf en Daube slowly cooked dish of marinated beef

17

Mrs Ramsay acts as hostess at the dinner party. She remains introspective, contemplating the meaning of her life, even as she presides over the gathering.

Lily Briscoe watches Mrs Ramsay with mixed emotions, her own current affection for William Bankes modifying the way she feels. Charles Tansley resents the triviality of the conversation. Mrs Ramsay reminisces with Bankes.

The conversation shifts to the fishing industry, although beneath that impersonal surface a variety of tensions and resentments are evident.

Candles are lit. Minta and Paul join the party. She explains that she has lost her brooch. Mr Ramsay chides her for wearing jewels on the beach, but he does so in a way that suggests to her that this man, like others, feels admiration for her looks. She is aware of her glow.

From that glow, Mrs Ramsay concludes that the couple are engaged to be married, and she feels, unexpectedly, jealous. The main course is brought in as Mrs Ramsay talks with Paul. Then she serves, choosing an especially tender piece of meat for William Bankes, who, in return, declares the dish a triumph.

Lily ponders love. Mrs Ramsay and Bankes talk of coffee and the dairy system. The family laugh at Mrs Ramsay's earnestness.

She thinks that Lily and Bankes should marry and determines to arrange a long walk or a picnic for them, to develop their relationship. She experiences a sense of stability and of eternity.

Charles Tansley takes issue with Bankes's taste for Sir Walter Scott's 'Waverley' novels. Mr Ramsay is in high spirits; he encourages Mr Carmichael to tell stories of a college acquaintance, and then they recite poetry. Mrs Ramsay rises from the table, takes Minta's arm, and they leave the room. She is aware that her dinner party has entered the past.

The dinner party depicted in this long section is a key event for Mrs Ramsay, as she draws people together despite their differences and despite the tensions between them. The dinner is a success that will remain in their memories. But her personal sense of triumph, as she presides over her domestic domain, is by no means straightforward. Lily Briscoe notes 'the complexity of things', and recognises that it is possible 'to feel violently two opposite things at the same time' (p. 95). Each of the participants looks at the shared event from their own particular point of view, and colours it with their own preoccupations. Virginia Woolf uses the occasion to illustrate the mixed nature of individual character and the instability of human relationships.

So soon after appearing to affirm her love for her husband, Mrs Ramsay here reflects that she cannot understand how she developed any attachment for him. She is overtaken by 'a sense of being past everything, through everything, out of everything' (p. 77). Yet she is immediately immersed in the dinner party. Her interior and exterior realities seem to have become radically separated. In the course of the dinner, however, they are reconciled as her introspection is balanced by the demands of her social role.

The role that she has assumed appears demanding: 'They all sat separate. And the whole of the effort of merging and flowing and creating rested on her' (p. 78). Other novelists might present the challenge facing the hostess as a matter for nervousness, but Virginia Woolf shows it to be a daunting struggle, requiring a concerted act of will. Because she places such emphasis in her characterisation upon interior states, this social occasion becomes the scene of a battle to overcome despair. Mrs Ramsay is not alone in confronting weighty questions. The scientist William Bankes asks himself, 'What does one live for?' (p. 83), and considers the frailty of friendship.

Mrs Ramsay has to establish a 'pulse' of hospitality, a rhythm that will temporarily bind her guests together. The pulse is compared to the ticking of a watch, but it is perhaps more apt to recall the pulsing of the Lighthouse beam, which Mrs Ramsay found so consoling in I, 11. Lily observes that Mrs Ramsay looks old, worn out, and remote, even as she is engaged in this process of social amalgamation. Amongst the strains that the older woman feels is a dispiriting sense of 'the sterility of men' (p. 78). Masculine attitudes, she perceives, tend to foster separation rather than unification.

Lily notes that Mrs Ramsay 'pitied men always as if they lacked something – women never, as if they had something' (p. 79). The hostess's clear-cut understanding of the differences between men and women involves unquestioning acceptance of her role as wife and mother, allowing her a fulfilment that she believes men cannot attain. Lily, unmarried and childless, is also denied access to that fulfilment. But Mrs Ramsay's troublesome doubts alert us to the fact that her fulfilment may be real on occasion, but is by no means continuously so. Lily Briscoe has an independence of spirit, which Virginia Woolf considered a positive advance on Mrs Ramsay's conservative acceptance of her allocated role.

The dinner party is ultimately a triumph for Mrs Ramsay, but Virginia Woolf does not indulge in sentimentality. Hostility and discontent lurk beneath the congenial surface. Charles Tansley smoulders with resentment towards women, who make 'civilisation impossible' (p. 80). Lily observes that Mr Tansley eats his meal with 'meagre fixity' and 'bare unloveliness' (p. 79). Mr Ramsay is furious when Mr Carmichael requests and is given a second bowl of soup. William Bankes feels uncomfortable, preferring to eat alone. He regards the party as a terrible waste of time, and longs to return to his work. Most devastatingly, Mrs Ramsay's 'presence meant absolutely nothing to him: her beauty meant nothing to him' (p. 83).

Each member of the group experiences an intense inner discourse beneath the surface conversation. The intensity of feeling amongst these adults is comparable to James's feelings of ire and bliss at the start of the novel. Tansley's underlying animosity towards Mrs Ramsay is compared to a hammer wielded to destroy a butterfly. Such feelings, it seems, do not go away at the onset of adulthood; they are merely placed under stricter control, in observance of social etiquette. The operation of such etiquette is illustrated through the example of a turbulent meeting, resolved through the chairman's decision that all present should speak French: 'Perhaps it is bad French; French may not contain the words that express the speaker's thoughts; nevertheless speaking French imposes some order, some uniformity' (pp. 83–4).

Speaking French at the meeting imposes a shared condition, which reduces the significance of differences among the participants. Polite conversation over dinner has a similar effect; what is said is less important than the fact that people speak with one another. More meaningful communication occurs through expressive glances and gestures. The Ramsays communicate in an especially intimate way, without need for speech: 'they looked at each other down the long table sending these questions and answers across, each knowing exactly what the other felt' (p. 89). Mrs Ramsay later considers 'those unclassified affections of which there are so many', signalling the inadequacy of language to classify and express the range of human feelings (p. 97).

While those around her discuss boots, Mrs Ramsay reaches a condition of security: 'she hovered like a hawk suspended; like a flag floated in an element of joy which filled every nerve of her body fully and sweetly' (p. 97). This is an example of Virginia Woolf's characteristically bold use of **simile**.

At this stage, despite the chatter around her, Mrs Ramsay feels: 'Nothing need be said; nothing could be said' (p. 97). It is a revelatory moment for her, transcending the trivial talk and the petty concerns of day-to-day living:

> there is a coherence in things, a stability; something, she meant, is immune from change, and shines out (she glanced at the window with its ripple of reflected lights) in the face of the flowing, the fleeting, the spectral, like a ruby (p. 97)

She has reached 'the still space that lies about the heart of things' (p. 98). She experienced a comparable sensation when contemplating the Lighthouse beam, in I, 11. But here she is not in isolation, but at the centre of a lively social gathering. The dinner party gels. It achieves a balanced composition, comparable to the achievement of an accomplished painter or novelist, resolving those tensions which have, up until this point, threatened formlessness and chaos: 'Of such moments, she thought, the thing is made that remains for ever after. This would remain' (p. 97).

Lily Briscoe feels similarly when, at the novel's conclusion, she completes her picture. In what sense might such moments be said to endure? Both women believe that they have granted form to life, which, in Virginia Woolf's view, is the most we can strive for. *To the Lighthouse* is itself an affirmation of the human capacity to bring order out of chaos. Whatever form the affirmation may take (dinner party, painting, novel or the scientific proofs cherished by William Bankes), it endures in the collective belief that human life can achieve coherence and purposefulness. Virginia Woolf wrote in the wake of the First World War, which seemed a huge negation, a denial of meaning, and an eruption of chaotic impersonal forces. Mrs Ramsay's dinner party, taking place before the war, was a small gain preceding the terrible loss. But it is a moment that remains with Lily as she completes her picture after the war, a frail but real bridge spanning that abyss.

Marlow a town in Buckinghamshire

Middlemarch novel, published in 1871–2, under the name George Eliot, a pseudonym assumed by Mary Ann Evans (1819–80)

the Mile End Road street in East London

Voltaire assumed name of François-Marie Arouet (1694–1778), satirical French author

Madame de Staël Germaine de Staël (1766–1817) French-Swiss writer of novels, plays, and critical essays

Lord Rosebery (1847–1929) Scottish Liberal politician, British Prime Minister during 1894–5

Creevey's Memoirs Thomas Creevey (1768–1838), English politician. An edition of his *Papers* was published in 1903, presenting Edwardian readers with a lively account of Georgian England

the Waverley novels series of historical novels by Sir Walter Scott (1771–1832)

Tolstoi Leo Nikolayevich Tolstoy (1828–1910), Russian novelist

Anna Karenina novel by Tolstoy, published in 1878

18

Lily watches as Bankes talks politics with Tansley. She then notices Mrs Ramsay going upstairs alone. Mrs Ramsay is envisaging Paul and Minta married. She enters the room where James and Cam should be sleeping, but both are still awake, and Mildred is talking with them, even though it is nearly eleven o'clock. Cam is upset by a boar's skull hanging on the wall, but James screams when Mildred tries to remove it. Mrs Ramsay wraps her shawl around the skull, and Cam is comforted by its modified appearance. She falls asleep.

James, however, remains awake, and asks about the trip to the Lighthouse. Mrs Ramsay replies realistically that they will not go tomorrow, but will do so on the next fine day. James then settles down to sleep, and Mrs Ramsay leaves the room.

The group below watches her as she stands on the stairs. Prue suggests going to the beach to watch the waves. Her mother, seeming suddenly youthful, encourages the young people to go. She would like to accompany them but feels unable to, and instead joins her husband, who is reading.

Lily notes that when Mrs Ramsay leaves the party a form of disintegration occurs. As an artist, she is especially interested in compositional unity, and recognises in Mrs Ramsay a centre of cohesion, holding diverse elements of the social grouping together, despite their differences.

Mrs Ramsay believes the occasion will endure as a moment of stability within the memory of those present: 'They would, she thought, going on again, however long they lived, come back to this night; this moon; this wind; this house: and to her too' (p. 105). She feels she has been woven into the hearts of these people, on account of:

> that community of feeling with other people which emotion gives as if the walls of partition had become so thin that practically (the feeling was one of relief and happiness) it was all one stream (p. 105)

After the moment of affirmation, a sense of mortality returns. The pig's skull acts as a reminder of death's inevitability, even though the younger Ramsay children are not fully aware of that significance. It is consistent with gender delineations in the book that the girl is troubled by the skull, while the boy takes pleasure in it. Cam's desire for concealment of the worrying object resembles her mother's efforts to disguise unpalatable truths in order to make life pleasant.

Cam projects images that please her on to the object, once its outline has been blurred. Compare how James was earlier seen to relish cutting out objects. He projected on to them, despite their distinctness, intense personal feelings, in contrast to Cam's imaginative embellishments. The distinction clearly delineates conventionally feminine and masculine responses. Yet while James seems bold in confronting the physical world, he is unable to sleep without a light. This may be seen as a parallel with the insecurity underlying Mr Ramsay's intellectual courage.

Towards the end of the dinner party, Mrs Ramsay felt warmth towards Charles Tansley; she now feels annoyed by him, and looks forward to his departure. Then she recognises that he has been admirable with her husband, and notes that his manners are improving. She does not have a single fixed view of him. Rather, her perception of Tansley shifts with her own shifting concerns. This emphasis upon variable perspective is an important aspect of Virginia Woolf's approach to characterisation (see Characterisation).

19

Mrs Ramsay resumes knitting while her husband reads a novel by Walter Scott. She too flicks through a book; then she observes how her husband draws strength from reading. They smile at one another, wordlessly communicating and sharing their experience, separate yet together.

Her mind ranges over the events of the day, real and imagined. Then, as she knits, she mentions the engagement of Paul and Minta. The Ramsays grow somehow closer together. Mrs Ramsay longs for her husband to speak, and he does so, seeking to counter the pessimism he perceives in her outlook. He wants her to say that she loves him. She is unable to do so, not because she does not feel that way, but because 'she never could say what she felt' (p. 114). He watches her as she looks at the Lighthouse. She is conscious of him looking. He is acutely aware of her beauty, and she feels herself beautiful. 'And as she looked at him she began to smile, for though she had not said a word, he knew, of course he knew, that she loved him'. In turn, she feels, 'Nothing on earth can equal this happiness' (p. 115).

> At the dinner party in I, 17, there was discussion of Walter Scott's novels. It turned Mr Ramsay's thoughts again to great men, their works and reputations, and Mrs Ramsay sensed her husband's 'extreme anxiety about himself' (p. 100). Here he reads Scott, and his wife recognises that in doing so he is conscious of the precariousness of his own reputation. Although she can understand his concern about public perception of himself and his books, she limits herself to domestic achievements and feels detached from his obsession with greatness.

> In I, 9 Lily conceived of herself as a bee visiting Mrs Ramsay, conceived as a hive. Here Mrs Ramsay herself, as she reads, is compared to a bee gathering nectar. Words lose distinct meaning to

become like sensations of colour: 'words, like little shaded lights, one red, one blue, one yellow, lit up in the dark of her mind' (p. 110). The novel persistently argues that language is an inadequate medium for conveying important aspects of human experience. Mrs Ramsay derives sensual pleasure from her encounter with words. This becomes possible when language is not subjected to a strictly functional demand that it carry a message. Virginia Woolf's own engagement with words had an evident aesthetic dimension; she did not just write to make a point, but attended to the shape and sound of sentences.

The Ramsays are reading literature, but Virginia Woolf continues to point out to us, as readers, that literature can only hint at certain forms of human experience which cannot be reduced to marks on paper. The Ramsays' eyes meet and without speaking they communicate something beyond verbal expression: 'They had nothing to say, but something seemed, nevertheless, to go from him to her' (p. 111).

The conclusion of 'The Window' is affirmative in showing this mutual love between the Ramsays, despite all the potential for disagreement, misunderstanding, and resentment. Mutuality is hard won in Virginia Woolf's novel, far more so than in conventional **realist fiction**. But, being hard won, it appears all the more valuable, and all the more worth striving for.

Mucklebackit's cottage Saunders Mucklebackit, a fisherman, appears in *The Antiquary* (1816) by Walter Scott
Balzac Honoré de Balzac (1799–1850), French novelist

The Ramsays and their guests go to sleep. Augustus Carmichael stays awake for a while, reading by candlelight. Time passes. Mrs Ramsay dies. The house falls into disrepair despite the efforts of Mrs McNab, the caretaker. Prue Ramsay marries, but dies not long afterwards of an illness connected with childbirth. Andrew Ramsay is killed fighting in the First World War. Mr Carmichael publishes a book of poetry, which is well received. The house is prepared for the return of the Ramsays, who bring with them Lily Briscoe and Augustus Carmichael

The first part of the novel ended with an affirmation of human values. In this much shorter second part, human beings appear increasingly insignificant as Virginia Woolf depicts the passage of time, manifested through the inexorable processes of the non-human world.

1

The voices of William Bankes, Andrew and Prue Ramsay, and Lily Briscoe are heard, and the lights in the house are extinguished. Mr Carmichael remains awake, reading by candlelight.

This brief section is continuous with the conclusion of the first part of the novel. The single day presented there comes to an end.

Virgil Publius Vergilius Maro (70–19BC), Roman epic poet, author of the *Aeneid*

2

A nocturnal scene: darkness has fallen and a thin rain falls. It is after midnight. Mr Carmichael stops reading and extinguishes his candle.

Virginia Woolf employs the metaphor of a flood engulfing the house to evoke the descent of darkness. The effect is a vivid rendering of transformation of the environment when the lights are extinguished. The familiar identities of individuals are subsumed into the undifferentiated darkness. Figures move or make sounds as they sleep, but their singularity has been lost. On the other hand, draughts of air passing through the rooms are **personified**, as if engaged in a process of deliberate investigation.

Virginia Woolf has avoided granting her narrative voice a distinct identity. It has not been linked to a particular person, and its flexible character does not suggest any single type of person. In 'The Window', it moved with ease between the various characters, passing smoothly from one consciousness to another, as well as registering events and objects in the external world. Now, as the characters sleep, the narrative creates a remarkable sense of a world free from the agitations of those individuals, with their thoughts and emotions, prejudices and obsessions. The characters we have come to recognise from the first part of the novel are consigned to terse, matter-of-fact **parenthetical** statements, contained in square brackets at the end of each section. The focus of our attention is shifted from the ripples on the surface to the unceasing, rolling force that generates the waves; we observe the processes of being, which are more fundamental than the experiences of individual lives.

3

The narrative voice broadens the focus from that specific night, following the dinner party, to the passage of time more generally, day following night, night following day.

Mrs Ramsay dies; her husband finds himself alone.

Winter is personified, shuffling nights like a deck of playing cards. The day presented in 'The Window' was one amongst many in the history of the world. Similarly, each individual character we have met is one amongst the multitude who have existed or will exist. In this section, our sense of time expands to accommodate the unfolding of history.

Nights become increasingly turbulent, suggesting perhaps the turbulent developments leading to the First World War. A concluding parenthetical statement announces starkly the sudden death of Mrs Ramsay. The effect is shocking. This is no impersonal loss in the historical record of some war, but a character with whom we have become intimately involved. Without warning she has gone, never to return. Her death is reported with detached neutrality and minimal detail. The contrast between the complexity of living and the blunt finality of death could scarcely have been rendered more emphatically. Yet Mrs Ramsay's life was one amongst very many, and life will continue in her absence.

Mr Ramsay is still stretching out his arms. As 'R' has eluded him in his philosophical quest, so too now does the body of his wife. He has lost the woman who, fulfilling her allocated role, provided his comfort amidst the darkness of the world. His childlike vulnerability is exposed once more.

The evocation of harvest moons recalls the particular moon that Mrs Ramsay observes in I, 18. The moon, especially during the phase signifying the fertility of harvest, has been traditionally associated with a feminine principle. Specific identification with Mrs Ramsay is strengthened here through reference to its 'light which mellows the energy of labour, and smooths the stubble, and brings the wave lapping blue to the shore' (p. 121). This is an effective summary, in **figurative** terms, of this woman's social role.

4

The empty house is described. There are faded skirts and coats which once held a human shape, and a looking glass that once framed a human face. The activity it once reflected has been irrevocably consigned to the past. Mrs McNab, at intervals as directed, opens windows and dusts the bedrooms.

> Mrs McNab, a character we have not met before, is introduced, and once again there is a human presence on the scene. Her task through subsequent sections will be to struggle to bring some form of orderliness to the abandoned and decaying house.

5

Mrs McNab, the coarse caretaker, nearly seventy years old, is described, cleaning the house.

Mrs McNab is a working-class woman, doing physical work of the kind Mrs Ramsay delegated to servants. Both women belong to the domestic sphere, and both seek to assert order against the constant threat of chaos. But the difference between their social class is blatant. Virginia Woolf's portrayal of Mrs McNab verges on caricature, especially when compared with her intricate and sensitive characterisation of Mrs Ramsay.

Another character, Charles Tansley, also has a working-class background. His uneasiness in middle-class company is evident in the hostility he feels towards Mrs Ramsay, on their walk and at the dinner party. Virginia Woolf came from an upper-middle-class background, and her attempts at characterisation beyond that milieu tend to be relatively unsatisfactory (see Historical Background – The General Strike).

6

The narrative voice speaks of spring. Prue Ramsay's marriage, in May, is mentioned. She died subsequently of illness connected with childbirth.

The narrative voice speaks lyrically of summer. There is further reference to Mrs McNab. We learn of the death of Andrew Ramsay, killed by a shell, while fighting in France.

Mr Carmichael publishes a book of poetry, which is successful.

The technique of **parenthetical** statement, which recorded Mrs Ramsay's death with such neutrality of tone, here reports the death of Prue, the most beautiful of the Ramsay girls. She married, but we do not know whom she married, only that her father gave her away. Sadness at her death is registered, although reported clinically, in language devoid of feeling: 'which was indeed a tragedy, people said. They said nobody deserved happiness more' (p. 126). The words employed appear particularly sterile following the carefully wrought poetical evocation of spring that opens this section.

The shock of Prue's death is followed with equally shocking reference to her brother Andrew's death in the war. The absence of emotional charge in the blunt language used to report this event heightens its impact. We have had access in 'The Window' to the consciousness of Mr Ramsay, and have seen the hopes he cherished for these two children in particular. Those aspirations have come to nothing. We may also recall the anxiety felt by Mrs Ramsay when Andrew returned late from the beach. Now, he is dead, blown up by a shell fired by a remote enemy. Each of these deaths reflects the nature of gender divisions in this novel: Prue dies as wife and mother; Andrew dies abroad, serving his country.

Reference is made in this section to men and women walking on the beach hoping to discover meaning in life. The harsh record of events, however, suggests that there is no grand design, and that reason, order and justice are dreams rather than realities. Certainly, in the war, as Mrs McNab says a little later, 'many families had lost their dearest' (p. 130). But if individual lives are lost in what seems an arbitrary manner, the pulse of being continues, the life of the world goes on. Virginia Woolf sought affirmation in that fact. She also wrote critically of the barbarous conduct of the First World War, which she recognised as a vivid sign that the governing patriarchy was ethically bankrupt. *Jacob's Room* (1922), *Mrs Dalloway* (1925), and this novel all engage in criticism of that patriarchal order, while searching for alternative means to discover value in the life of post-war Europe.

It seems **ironic** that while the young die Augustus Carmichael flourishes. Indeed, it appears almost perverse that while the Ramsays' hopes were invested in young people who no longer exist, it is the old man whose life seemed to have receded into the past as he lay on the lawn, somnolent, who has acted creatively and received recognition. Virginia Woolf seems to be making an important point through this eccentric figure. Prue followed her mother into marriage and pregnancy, and died. Andrew took the conventionally masculine path and went to war, and died. Carmichael quietly yet assiduously produced poetry; he has survived and has created a bridge to other people. Art, which Carmichael's old friend Ramsay rejected as embellishment, Virginia Woolf saw as essential to the restoration of human value within a badly damaged culture.

7

A description of summer and winter storms. The scene around the unoccupied house is turbulent. Spring brings bright days, but there are no human eyes to witness them.

> The narrative voice articulates the scene. This description of the natural world, in the absence of an identifiable human consciousness, may remind us of the central concern of Mr Ramsay's philosophy, summarised by Andrew in his exhortation to Lily Briscoe: 'Think of a kitchen table then ... when you're not there' (p. 21).

8

Mrs McNab picks flowers from the garden, aware that the Ramsay family will probably not return to the island. It has been years since their last visit. The war and consequent travel restrictions seem partly to blame for this neglect. It is rumoured that the house is to be sold. It has fallen into disrepair. Books have become mouldy. The garden is overgrown. Years have passed since Mrs Ramsay's death, and moths have attacked her clothes.

Mrs McNab recalls how she brought washing to the house, was greeted by Mrs Ramsay, and enjoyed a laugh with the fiery cook, red-haired Mildred. But now those days have passed, never to return. Upkeep of the house is too demanding for one old woman. She locks the house and departs.

> Mrs Ramsay lives on in the memory of Mrs McNab. She is perpetuated, but in a way that has very evident limits. It requires artistry to transcend those limits, and keep a more faithful and sensitive memory alive. Virginia Woolf has created Mrs Ramsay within a work of literary art, and in doing so she has made her own memory of her mother Julia Stephen an enduring element in literary history.

> Mr Ramsay is obsessed with his own reputation as an author of philosophical works, and he repeatedly considers the public fate of

writers such as Walter Scott and William Shakespeare. There is typical egotism in his concern. Carmichael's poems seem an unselfish communication by comparison. Virginia Woolf regarded her books as gifts, rather than as reflections of self, or testimony to her personal greatness.

9

The abandoned and decaying house is described. Nature has begun to colonise it, in the absence of human occupants.

At length, Mrs McNab returns, accompanied by her friend Mrs Bast. They set to work, attempting to clean and tidy the place, in anticipation of a visit from the Ramsays. Mrs McNab reminisces, uncertain whether it was Mrs or Mr Ramsay who died. Mrs Bast was living in Glasgow during the days of the Ramsays' residency. Her son, George Bast, attends to the garden. Their collective efforts manage to restore some order to the house, prior to the arrival, in September, of the Ramsays, Lily Briscoe, and Augustus Carmichael.

The name Bast possibly alludes to Leonard Bast, a working-class character in the novel *Howards End* (1910), by Virginia Woolf's friend E.M. Forster.

10

The war ends and peace returns. Lily lies in bed in the house, listening to the waves and 'the voice of the beauty of the world' (p. 135). In addition to Mr Carmichael, Mrs Beckwith, an old lady who sketches, is staying. As sleep approaches, Mr Carmichael feels that all is much as it was. Next morning, Lily, on awakening, is self-conscious about her presence in the house.

The war has come and gone. Despite its horrific consequences, the life of the world goes on, and Lily Briscoe, the artist, finds affirmation in the pleasure of being in this place. Carmichael, the poet, perceives continuity despite the lapse of time and the intervening historical trauma.

**Mr Ramsay takes James and Cam on a boat-trip to the Lighthouse.
Lily Briscoe works on her painting, and at last manages to complete it**

1

Lily Briscoe, now forty-four years old, is at the breakfast table.
Mr Ramsay, Cam and James have arranged an expedition to the
Lighthouse. The young Ramsays are not ready, and their father is furious.
James, now sixteen, and his sister, a year older, are not enthusiastic about
the trip, but their father has coerced them.

Nancy asks Lily's advice concerning what gifts to send to the
Lighthouse. Feeling curiously detached from the place and the moment,
Lily is unable to respond to this simple enquiry. Following the deaths of
Mrs Ramsay, Andrew and Prue she feels this situation to be 'aimless',
'chaotic' and 'unreal'.

Lily determines to complete the picture she left unfinished on her
previous visit. She feels that she is merely playing at painting, but at the
same time considers a paintbrush to be 'the one dependable thing in a
world of strife, ruin, chaos' (p. 143).

Ten years have elapsed since the day depicted in 'The Window'.
The brief 'Time Passes' spans more than a decade.

The novel's thematic concern with the inadequacy of language to
express important aspects of life is pursued further in 'The
Lighthouse'. Lily Briscoe becomes the principal voice calling words
into question. Pondering her feelings on returning to the island so
long after Mrs Ramsay's death, she finds there is 'Nothing, nothing
– nothing that she could express at all' (p. 139).

Characters do continue to speak, however. Mr Ramsay utters the
words 'Alone' and 'Perished'. Hearing them, Lily feels they are
transformed by the context and the circumstances, so that 'like
everything else this strange morning the words became symbols,
wrote themselves all over the grey-green walls' (p. 140). Lily's desire
is to marry the fragments together, in order to discover in wholeness
the meaning of life: 'If only she could put them together, she felt,
write them out in some sentence, then she would have got at the

truth of things' (pp. 140–1). It becomes increasingly clear in this part of the novel that Lily discerned a capacity for synthesis in Mrs Ramsay's approach to living, and she seeks to emulate her, not as wife and mother, but as artist.

Lily decides to finish the picture she started on her previous visit to the island: 'It seemed as if the solution had come to her: she knew now what she wanted to do' (p. 141). Mrs Ramsay's lesson has been transmitted across the intervening years. Lily adopts the same physical position as in 'The Window'. But just as, years before, Mr Ramsay had disrupted his wife's efforts to establish domestic order and calm, so now he hinders the completion of Lily's picture.

Mr Ramsay is characterised as a man who takes but never gives; his wife was a giver, and so is Lily Briscoe. Lily paints not to acquire a reputation for greatness, but to make a gift for others. Virginia Woolf would have recognised a feminist orientation in this generosity and lack of presumption. Lily draws inspiration from recollection of Mrs Ramsay, and from the 'self-surrender' of other women, who blazed 'into a rapture of sympathy' which 'evidently conferred on them the most supreme bliss of which human nature was capable' (p. 144). Sympathy being an effective bridge between people, Lily decides to give Mr Ramsay whatever support she can, recognising how dependent upon his wife he has been.

Although Lily feels enormously inspired by Mrs Ramsay's example as a 'giver', her affection for the older woman is not unalloyed. She experiences moments of resentment at her absence. Her death has left an uncomfortably empty space on the step, where she used to sit. Virginia Woolf's characterisation remains complex. It requires an affirmative action to cancel the effect of such tensions.

2

Mr Ramsay notes changes in Lily. He is drawn to her, as a woman, by his need for sympathetic attention, but Lily is unable to respond with appropriate expansiveness. Ramsay groans, and sighs; Lily feels herself to be 'not a woman, but a peevish, ill-tempered, dried-up old maid' (p. 145).

Ramsay makes it clear that the trip to the Lighthouse is intended as a form of homage to his wife. His agitated presence clouds Lily's perception of the world, even of Mr Carmichael, who is reading contentedly nearby.

Lily praises Ramsay's boots. He smiles, and the discomfort of the moment passes, just as James and Cam arrive, looking melancholy. They troop off, preparing for the expedition. The gate bangs, announcing their departure.

Despite her resolution in the previous section, Lily finds it difficult to extend sympathy on a personal basis, especially to a man like Ramsay.

The narrative voice shifts between the points of view of these two characters. It is clear that Mr Ramsay wants Lily to offer sympathetic support, as his wife did. He assumes she will do so, simply because she is a woman. But Lily does not conform to type: she is an artist, not a wife and mother. In making that choice she is not, as Mr Ramsay would see it, going against her nature, but is rejecting restrictive conventions established within patriarchal society.

Praising Ramsay's boots, which he prizes, proves enough to raise his spirits: 'They had reached, she felt, a sunny island where peace dwelt, sanity reigned and the sun for ever shone, the blessed island of good boots' (p. 147). Boots were discussed by the men at the dinner party in 'The Window', while Mrs Ramsay experienced a sense of connection with eternity. For all his concern with issues of public greatness, Ramsay finds contentment in boots, and as he ties Lily's shoe, he seems to her 'a figure of infinite pathos' (p. 147).

Still, when his children appear, Ramsay reverts to the role of a dignified elderly man. In I, 6 his personal strengths were compared to those of a heroic ship's captain, and a polar explorer. A truer picture now emerges as we see him organising an expedition to the local Lighthouse. The qualities required for this may be of the same order, but they are clearly not of the same scale. The heroism conventionally associated with masculine values is accordingly diminished.

Virginia Woolf uses a **parenthetical** remark, '(He had been killed by the splinter of a shell instantly, she bethought her.)' (p. 148), to show the working of involuntary memory. A process of association brings Andrew Ramsay's death to Lily's thoughts momentarily. The nature of Andrew's death may be seen as further diminution of masculine heroism. In Tennyson's poem 'The Charge of the Light Brigade', which Mr Ramsay recites almost continuously in 'The Window', the death of soldiers, resulting from a blunder, appears glorious. No such gloss can be put on the death of Andrew Ramsay, who is not a faceless fighter, but a gifted individual and a loved son, destroyed in a bleakly impersonal, profoundly inglorious modern war.

3

Lily is left alone, on the lawn, with her painting. She remembers Charles Tansley watching her paint on her previous visit. She also recalls playing the stone-throwing game 'ducks and drakes' with him, on the beach, while Mrs Ramsay looked on. Lily asks herself the simple yet momentous question, 'What is the meaning of life?' (p. 153). She realises that she has had no great revelation, but 'Instead there were little daily miracles, illuminations, matches struck unexpectedly in the dark' (p. 154).

She walks to the end of the lawn, and sees, in the distance, a small boat which she decides is the one bearing Mr Ramsay and his children. Its sail is raised, and it moves out to sea.

> The mixed nature of human response is again explicitly acknowledged. Lily feels both relief and disappointment at the departure of the Ramsays: 'She felt curiously divided, as if one part of her were drawn out there' (p. 149).
>
> She attends to her painting, which she has regularly wrestled with, conceptually, since her last visit. She has come to recognise that the physical act of painting is quite distinct from abstract planning: 'All that in idea seemed simple became in practice immediately complex' (p. 150). This statement, applied to the painting, can equally be applied to Virginia Woolf's overall understanding of life. Scientists and philosophers can produce elegantly coherent abstract

models, but actually engaging with human life remains intensely problematic. It was this engagement that Mrs Ramsay achieved. Her husband still struggles to develop his philosophical model.

Lily recognises that any mark made on the canvas 'committed her to innumerable risks, to frequent and irrevocable decisions' (p. 150). Living is difficult in practice, more difficult than the most abstruse philosophy.

The work of artists, exemplified by Lily Briscoe, is extolled as an immersion in the world, shunning the sterility of abstraction. Mr Ramsay's rejection of art as mere embellishment is emphatically rebuffed. In using the word 'strokes' to describe Lily's acts of painting, Virginia Woolf may be using a deliberate **pun** to recall the Lighthouse whose strokes beat across the island, assisting Mrs Ramsay's efforts to establish a sense of contact with the real world beyond the self.

There are further parallels to that passage in I, 11 where Mrs Ramsay senses a wedge-shaped core of darkness within herself. Lily Briscoe is

drawn out of gossip, out of living, out of community with people into the presence of this formidable ancient enemy of hers – this other thing, this truth, this reality, which suddenly laid hands on her, emerged stark at the back of appearances and commanded her attention. (p. 151)

The struggle commences when Lily prepares to exchange 'the fluidity of life for the concentration of painting' (p. 151). It is described as a moment of vulnerability, when departure from the securities of routine results in lowering of the defences of the self. Lily loses 'consciousness of outer things, and her name and her personality and her appearance' (p. 152). Her experience of the act of painting dissolves the familiar distinction between subject and object (see Theme on Subject and Object and the Nature of Reality).

Lily senses that her painting will not be valued. It will be hung in a servant's bedroom or stored away. It will not add her name to the list of great men preoccupying Mr Ramsay. But that is not important to her; it is a conventionally masculine concern, and she aligns herself rather with Mrs Ramsay's intimate affirmation of order: 'In the midst of chaos there was shape; this eternal passing and flowing (she looked at the clouds going and the leaves shaking) was struck into stability' (p. 154). Both women work without egotism, and reach their goals, while the self-obsessed Ramsay struggles in vain to advance his philosophy from Q to R.

playing ducks and drakes a game of skimming stones on the surface of water. The familiar gendered name of the game is apt, given the novel's use of stereotypical masculine and feminine values

4

Mr Ramsay sits impatiently in the middle of a small sailing boat, crewed by the owner, Macalister and his boy. James steers and Cam sits in the bow; both are resentful at being compelled to make the trip against their will. Both hope the expedition will fail.

Once they are underway, Ramsay smokes his pipe and chats with Macalister. The experience of the sea inspires him to start reciting again, although he is hampered by self-consciousness. He draws his children's attention to the island. Ramsay tests Cam on the points of the compass. In answer to another question, she tells him that her brother Jasper is looking after their puppy. He asks the name of the dog, but Cam does not answer.

Ramsay is perceived as a tyrant by his teenage children, despite the fact that he conceives the voyage to the Lighthouse as homage to their mother. They view him as a classic patriarch, enjoying the sight of men labouring:

pitting muscle and brain against the waves and the wind; he liked men to work like that, and women to keep house, and sit beside sleeping children indoors, while men were drowned out there in a storm. (p. 157)

Cam's ignorance of the compass points prompts her father to dwell on the vagueness of women, which he believes forms part of their charm. Once again he readily derives a general case from a specific instance, regarding it as evidence of the essential nature of women.

Ramsay's conservative view fits squarely with the Victorian notion of separate public and domestic spheres, the former for men, the latter for women. Virginia Woolf felt that division had been rendered finally untenable by the First World War, where the horrors faced by men fighting in the public arena were paralleled by terrible losses inflicted on their families back home (see Theme on Social Criticism). It was also a war that disclosed generational differences, the older generation sacrificing the young upon the altar of outmoded values. In the next section, Lily declares that 'Life has changed completely' since Mrs Ramsay's day (p. 166).

The simple question concerning their puppy becomes a battleground between the children and their father. Cam especially is aware of 'pressure and division of feeling' in her relationship to the old man and her compact with her brother. She loves her father, while resenting 'that crass blindness and tyranny of his which had poisoned her childhood and raised bitter storms' (p. 161).

Still, Cam sees her father as 'brave' and 'adventurous' (p. 157). In I, 6 the description of Mr Ramsay's character suggests that he has the qualities of a heroic adventurer, but such an elevated term seems **ironic** when applied to this trip. Mr Ramsay, who always insists on the importance of facts, here indulges in self-dramatisation, indicating that the processes of his mind are as reliant upon the weaving of fictions as are those of the most imaginative person. The extent of this imaginative dimension of reality, which forms much of the substance of Virginia Woolf's art, is not acknowledged by Ramsay's philosophy.

Virginia Woolf explores the effect of difference in point of view both through technique and as a theme. Mr Ramsay points out to Cam the way their familiar holiday home has receded into the distance and consequently appears strange. The appearance of objects we perceive changes depending on where we stand, and our sense of their reality changes accordingly. Cam feels the realness of the boat on the sea, but the island, where she once picked flowers, seems unreal to her.

But I beneath a rougher sea ... from 'The Castaway', a poem by William Cowper (1731–1800)

5

Lily watches the boat which, she has decided, carries the Ramsays. She feels that she has failed Mr Ramsay by withholding her sympathy. She turns to her painting, attending to the issue of perspective.

Lily recalls Paul and Minta Rayley, whose marriage 'turned out rather badly' (p. 164), although all was rectified when Paul took a mistress.

Lily ponders the loss of Mrs Ramsay, her absence and the inadequacy of language to express important aspects of human experience. She poses to herself the fundamental questions: 'What does it mean? How do you explain it all?' (p. 170).

Lily senses the possibility of a kind of telepathic communication with Mr Carmichael. She imagines the old man saying that all earthly things must pass, but consoles herself with the thought that writing and painting can endure, even if neglected, as she suspects her own will be.

Lily finds that she is crying. She feels that the world offers no guidance. Rather, it involves a continual leap into the unknown. She craves an explanation, or, still better, the return of Mrs Ramsay.

Virginia Woolf was fascinated by the way certain elements of memory float involuntarily to the surface of one's recollection. Recalling Mrs Ramsay on the beach, Lily muses:

Why, after all these years had that survived, ringed round, lit up, visible to the last detail, with all before it blank and all after it blank, for miles and miles? (pp. 162–3)

Value attaches to seemingly insignificant details, the kind of details that form so much of the substance of Virginia Woolf's fiction.

Memory was a major concern for the great French novelist Marcel Proust (1871–1922). Lily describes her aim in doing a painting:

Beautiful and bright it should be on the surface, feathery and evanescent, one colour melting into another like the colours on a butterfly's wing; but beneath the fabric must be clamped together with bolts of iron. (p. 163)

The terms employed here closely resemble those used by Virginia Woolf in her diary to describe the structuring of Proust's work. The image here corresponds to that of the waves, continuous below while fragmented on the surface.

Lily recalls a hole in the heel of Minta Doyle's stocking and speculates that in the mind of William Bankes it would have stood **metonymically** for 'the annihilation of womanhood, and dirt and disorder' (p. 164). Virginia Woolf's perception that an entire world-view may hinge upon such a detail explains the meticulous focus upon such details so notable in her fiction.

Lily recalls the Rayleys in a series of scenes:

> this making up scenes about them, is what we call "knowing" people, "thinking" of them, "being fond" of them! Not a word of it was true; she had made it up; but it was what she knew them by all the same. (pp. 164–5)

Acts of fictional composition, dramatising the world around us and the people we meet, form the basis for knowing, as well as being the basic technique of the novelist. We all continually weave stories around the people, places, and things in our lives, and our sense of self also is caught up in the storytelling web. The writer becomes, in that light, a representative human being, raising to self-awareness the fundamental processes by which we achieve a sense of comprehending reality.

The same person can feature very differently in stories woven by different people. Lily recognises that the dead 'are at our mercy' (p. 166), we can treat their memory as we wish. Mr Ramsay's sense of his wife differs in significant ways from Lily Briscoe's perception of her, or from Charles Tansley's. Yet there will also be intersections, points in common that link the differing versions of who Mrs Ramsay was. She had, of course, her own version (or versions) of the real Mrs Ramsay.

Lily remembers Mrs Ramsay resting 'in silence, uncommunicative'. She speaks of 'the extreme obscurity of human relationships', and she asks: 'Who knows what we are, what we feel? Who knows even at the moments of intimacy, This is knowledge?' (p. 163). Mrs Ramsay cherished the expressiveness of silence, and knew that words could break apart a hard-won sense of life's wholeness. Such an understanding of the precariousness of what we call knowledge of other people informs Virginia Woolf's approach to characterisation, making it strikingly different to that found in conventional **realist fiction**

Lily notes Mrs Ramsay's 'mania ... for marriage' (p. 167), and clearly feels proud that by not marrying she has established independence from her friend's old-fashioned prejudices. She even considers how she would have felt triumphant telling her old friend that the marriage between Minta Doyle and Paul Rayley, which Mrs Ramsay had supported so ardently, had failed. She also hoped for a wedding between Lily and William Bankes. It never happened, but Lily admits that 'his friendship had been one of the pleasures of her life. She loved William Bankes.' A crucial element of their friendship was that 'Many things were left unsaid' (p. 168).

Raphael (1483–1520) is famed for his depiction of the Madonna and Child

Hampton Court palace near London, built by Cardinal Wolsey (1475–1530), and given by him to Henry VIII

a blade would be flashed alluding to the sword Excalibur in Arthurian legend. Tennyson describes its emergence from a lake in 'Morte d'Arthur' (1842)

6

Macalister's boy cuts a piece from a living fish to bait his hook, and throws the fish into the sea.

The boy cutting the fish is an example of masculine activity being associated with sharp instruments. Sometimes it is a **figurative** association, suggesting the analytical capacity of masculine reasoning. Here it is literal, indicating a capacity for detachment while harming another creature. The boy's equanimity while mutilating the fish may recall Jasper's callousness when shooting at birds. The suggestion is that men are trained into such detachment.

7

Lily, in her anguish, calls out to the absent Mrs Ramsay. She returns to her painting, envisaging her lost friend by means of 'some trick of the painter's eye' (p. 172). Even in central London, Lily has experienced a vision of Mrs Ramsay being escorted across fields by the shadowy figure of Death.

She sees the boat carrying the Ramsays, halfway across the bay.

Mrs Ramsay looms large in Lily's memory. In III, 5 Lily recognised that the dead 'are at our mercy' (p. 166), we can treat their memory as we wish. The image of Mrs Ramsay being escorted across fields by Death, which arises in Lily's imaginative mind, suggests a treatment of her memory that is closer to **myth** than to history. The considerable importance which Mrs Ramsay has assumed for the younger woman is not diminished with the passing of time.

Lily, surveying the bay, perceives all to be part of the same fabric, sea and sky, ships and cliffs. Like Mrs Ramsay, Lily has a capacity for synthesis, drawing together and connecting separate elements.

8

Cam, on the boat, feels that life on the shore is unreal. The breeze drops and the boat is becalmed, miles from both shore and Lighthouse. The space seems frozen.

Mr Ramsay reads a book. James is tense. He considers his relationship to his father, the animosity but also the closeness. He recalls the childhood frustration and fury of the incident that opened the novel. Then he looks at the Lighthouse and contemplates the nature of its reality. He recalls his mother.

The wind rises again and the boat moves towards the Lighthouse.

James's recollection takes us back to the novel's opening, and his initial extreme response to his father's negativity. The image of the blade, associated with masculine aggression, recurs **figuratively**: 'He had always kept this old symbol of taking a knife and striking his father to the heart' (p. 175). Resentment at Mr Ramsay's authoritarian presence leaves James feeling that whatever career awaits him, he will always oppose tyranny. But after considering his father's various moods, James acknowledges their closeness and their intimate knowledge of one another. This complex response is typical of Virginia Woolf's approach to character. Responses do not conform to a simple cause-and-effect pattern.

James's crucial insight is that 'nothing was simply one thing' (p. 177). Even a simple object can assume another reality when perceived from an alternative point of view. For James, there are two Lighthouses: the stark physical presence, and the image seen distantly across the bay. The object has a physical existence for all to witness, but it also resides as an object of perception within each individual's consciousness. Remember that in I, 4 Lily Briscoe experiences two particular sensations while talking with William Bankes: in one, all she herself feels subjectively about him is concentrated; in the other, she apprehends the objective existence of the man himself. It is the case with human beings, as well as with inanimate objects, that 'nothing [is] simply one thing'.

9

A brief **parenthetical** section presents Lily's view of the scene at sea. The sailing vessels have disappeared from view, becoming 'part of the nature of things' (p. 179).

Lily muses that 'Distance had an extraordinary power' (p. 179). The observation resonates on a number of accounts. The Lighthouse captivated James at the start of the novel because its remoteness made it an object of desire, rather than of familiarity. Similarly, foreign locations assume an exotic aspect for Mrs Ramsay, for Lily and for Cam because they are distant from their own experience. Also, the word love signifies, amongst other things, a craving for nearness to a loved one. Separation is painful for lovers; distance creates longing. So, when Mrs Ramsay dies, her husband continues to reach out for her.

10

Cam notes the appearance of the island from the sea; it looks very small. She recalls Mr Carmichael and Mr Bankes, two old men in conversation, while her father wrote at a desk nearby. In his study, she thinks, her father seems both lovable and wise, not the vain tyrant he becomes elsewhere.

She murmurs a line of poetry, much loved by her father, concerning how we each perish alone.

> Cam tells herself 'a story of adventure about escaping from a sinking ship'. She wants 'the sense of adventure' (p. 179). Narratives of adventure at the time Virginia Woolf wrote were invariably tales of masculine heroism. Cam, wild as a child, now relishes escape from domesticity, and feels elated at being alive. It is an 'unthinking fountain of joy', but it shapes her dreams of 'Greece, Rome, Constantinople' (p. 180). This desire to visit exotic places illustrates Lily's point, in the preceding section, that distance has extraordinary power. Mrs Ramsay made only imaginary journeys to India and Rome, obliged as she was to stay at home; but it seems unlikely that Cam, who belongs to another generation, will accept domestic confinement so readily.

11

Lily, trying to address the challenge posed by her picture, considers how distance between people can alter their relationship, their sense of one another. She thinks of Mr Carmichael's aloofness and the impersonality of his poetry. Carmichael felt distaste, she thinks, for Mrs Ramsay's directness. She considers more generally the criticisms people probably levelled at Mrs Ramsay. She conceives that her friend had 'an instinct like the swallows for the south, the artichokes for the sun, turning her infallibly to the human race, making her nest in its heart' (pp. 186–7). Her assuredness unsettled other people, including Lily herself. Lily imagines tensions within the Ramsays' marriage.

Someone enters the drawing room and sits down, casting a shadow that fits the composition of Lily's incomplete picture. Is it a projection of

Mrs Ramsay in Lily's imagination? Her mind turns to Mr Ramsay, on the boat, and she feels she wants to be with him.

Lily's musings at this point recall Mrs Ramsay achieving a moment of peace while contemplating the Lighthouse beam, in I, 11. Importantly, she realises that 'One need not speak at all'. Throughout the animate world, human and non-human, she senses 'some common feeling which held the whole together'. It is a 'feeling of completeness' redolent of Mrs Ramsay's example (p. 183).

But in Virginia Woolf's fiction the world is never at rest, and Lily's contentment is soon superseded by 'an obscure distress' (p. 183). The painting provides a focus for that distress:

It was a miserable machine, an inefficient machine, she thought, the human apparatus for painting and for feeling; it always broke down at the critical moment; heroically, one must force it on. (p. 184)

Mr Ramsay, in the boat, indulges in self-dramatisation; now Lily conceives of the artistic enterprise as heroic endeavour. But there are important differences in their sense of self.

The simile which affirms that:

a traveller, even though he is half asleep, knows, looking out of the train window, that he must look now, for he will never see that town, or that mule-cart, or that woman at work in the fields, again. (p. 184)

recalls the passage in I, 6 where, in a simile designed to shed light on Mr Ramsay's outlook, reference is made to the act of looking out of a train window, and finding in the world outside confirmation of something written on the printed page (p. 31).

Ramsay seeks support for his own authority, while Lily values the experience in itself. They are united in their love for Mrs Ramsay, and the love felt by each is genuine. But Ramsay invariably sought sympathetic support in return, whereas Lily is content to accept Mrs Ramsay's example of drawing fragments of reality into some form of wholeness.

Recollection of Charles Tansley preaching brotherly love during wartime illustrates that man's blinkered vision. His political objection to the war was doubtless fuelled by his sense that it was a dreadful exploitation of working-class men. But Lily recognises that Tansley's attitudes towards women, and towards art, are inimical to the development of real fellow-feeling of the kind that might prevent societies engaging in the destructiveness of warfare.

Mrs Ramsay, on the other hand, was expansive in her attempts to generate love and encourage mutual understanding. Her openness to life is the orientation sought by Lily in her approach to painting:

> One wanted, she thought, dipping her brush deliberately, to be on a level with ordinary experience, to feel simply that's a chair, that's a table, and yet at the same time, It's a miracle, it's an ecstasy. (p. 192)

Both women reject the conventionally masculine desire to control and manipulate the world, opting instead 'to be on a level with ordinary experience'.

12

Mr Ramsay, on the boat, is watched by his son James. They approach the Lighthouse. Ramsay closes his book, and they eat lunch prior to arrival. Two men await them. The Ramsays, carrying parcels, alight on the rock.

For James, his father represents 'that loneliness which was for both of them the truth about things'. It is a state encapsulated for him by the image of 'a stark tower on a bare rock' (p. 193). This belief in ultimate isolation stands in stark contrast to the efforts made by Mrs Ramsay to overcome loneliness and form bonds between people. Yet it is in homage to her that the trip has been made, bearing gifts for the lighthouse-keepers. The separating distance has in effect been cancelled by their action, and a bridge of sympathy has been extended from the mainland to the Lighthouse.

James sustains a sense that he and his sister, Cam, are united in their opposition to their father's tyranny. In fact, he is fundamentally aligned to his father's position, growing towards that conventional masculine role envisaged for him by his mother on the first page of the novel. Cam perceives the disingenuousness of her brother's feigned indifference to praise received from his father.

Macalister points out the site of a wreck where three men drowned. Mr Ramsay accepts that men die in that way, the consequence of taking risks, an integral part of masculine enterprise. Immediately afterwards, he appears to engage in a mathematical calculation, as if to confirm the alignment of the mathematical mind with other masculine values. His tendency to regard gender characteristics as natural rather than conventional means that, even after the war, he cannot conceive of human behaviour outside the conservative framework of patriarchal values.

Ramsay is long-sighted; Cam (like her mother) is near-sighted. There is a **figurative** as well as a literal significance in this distinction. The conventionally masculine perspective is detached to the point of remoteness; the conventionally feminine perspective pays intimate attention to details.

13

Lily thinks of Mr Ramsay arriving at the Lighthouse. Mr Carmichael concurs with her sense that the trio have reached their goal. She completes her painting with a single, crucial brush-stroke.

Lily's effort to draw the Lighthouse into relationship with her immediate environment combines evidence of the senses with workings of the imagination. It is not a process of abstraction, but a creative bridging of the physical distance separating her from Mr Ramsay and his children. Her concern for him is the realisation of that sympathy he had earlier demanded from her, but it does not pander to his masculine egotism.

Lily feels that she has a kind of telepathic communication with Augustus Carmichael, who seems to be thinking along the same lines as her. She imagines his poetry to be impersonal; it is work that springs from a man's experience of the world, not a woman's. Still, he has created, and has made contact with other people. Just as she earlier conceived Mrs Ramsay in mythical terms, Lily now perceives the old poet as a benign and compassionate pagan god. In those terms, he seems to pre-date the scientific world-view that constrains Mr Ramsay, whose obsession with stark facts hinders his engagement with human truths.

Lily experiences a vision of completeness which enables her to finish her picture, drawing its components into harmonious relationship through a single stroke of the brush. The fate of the picture may be to hang in attics but, crucially, Lily has not only embraced a principle of seeking to draw harmony, wholeness and stability out of the world's chaos, but has acted upon it. For Virginia Woolf that was the most to which an artist could aspire. Mrs Ramsay has gone, irretrievably, but the example she set has bridged that final gap, and has touched the artist at work.

PART THREE

CRITICAL APPROACHES

CHARACTERISATION

In conventional **realist fiction**, the writer aims to enable readers to feel that they know the characters. There may be some elements of mystery in the characterisation, but they invariably add momentum to the **plot**, and eventually all is resolved and made clear. In Virginia Woolf's fiction, characterisation is altogether less straightforward. Presentation of individual characters highlights contradiction, and human nature appears to be a mixture of conflicting impulses, held in uneasy tension. Motivation often remains obscure, even to the character involved. Speech, which in realist fiction usually acts as a reliable indicator of feelings, is in Virginia Woolf's work usually detached from inner states, and may appear at odds with them.

For centuries, European literature presented self-knowledge as the crucial form of wisdom. Virginia Woolf's characters have little hope of achieving such privileged understanding. The self is too elusive and too complex to be encapsulated in any handy verbal formula; it is volatile, changing constantly in response to slight alterations in the environment, or to modified circumstances.

But there are some relatively constant elements. Her characters cling to certain obsessions, which recur in their thoughts and appear through their actions. Memories, generally linked to these obsessions, but often arising involuntarily, provide some sense of continuity through time. Also, each character exists within the consciousness of other characters. So, we see Mrs Ramsay through her own thoughts, utterances and actions, and we see her as she exists for her husband, Lily Briscoe, Charles Tansley and Mr Carmichael. Their responses vary from one to another, however, and each has the potential to swing wildly from love to loathing.

Her approach to characterisation makes Virginia Woolf's work seem difficult when first encountered, but is also central to her artistic success. She presented character in this oblique way because she recognised that life is like that, even though most novels incline to simplify its complexity, artificially stabilising radically unstable elements of human existence. Virginia Woolf aspired to produce a higher form of realism, which necessitated forgoing the kind of ready knowledge upon which realism conventionally depended. The predictable, explicable world offered by most previous novels was, she felt, illusory. In the modern world of the early twentieth century, life was recognised as more complex, less certain, more challenging. Virginia Woolf felt that literary art had to be responsive to that complexity, uncertainty and challenge.

Immense skill was required, given her approach to characterisation, to avoid formlessness. A prop that Virginia Woolf employed to help her handle character was a schematic division of gender characteristics and roles. There is a clear demarcation in *To the Lighthouse* of masculine and feminine domains. The masculine domain is the public realm where significant contributions to society are made, and historical decisions are taken. The feminine realm is the home, where Mrs Ramsay acts as wife and mother.

Gender definition plays a major role in shaping attitudes and directing behaviour. Virginia Woolf's use of that definition is schematic, but it is also highly critical. Mr and Mrs Ramsay largely conform to type, but Lily Briscoe and Augustus Carmichael, the painter and the poet, signal the inadequacy of conventional roles. Moreover, allusion in the novel to the historical disaster of the First World War suggests that the dominance of conventionally masculine values has reached an impasse. Virginia Woolf subtly articulates a feminist position (see Theme on Social Criticism).

Elements for the characterisation of Mr and Mrs Ramsay were derived from Virginia Woolf's parents, Leslie and Julia Stephen. The novelist felt that her mother, whose physical beauty was widely acknowledged, was a steady, calming influence in her childhood. But she felt that Mrs Stephen lived too easily within the limits imposed by her status as an upper-middle-class woman. Virginia Woolf's father was a respected public figure, a man whom she loved when she saw him at work in his study, yet he could be a tyrant in the home.

The complexity of Virginia Woolf's characterisation should be borne in mind when reading the summaries of the main characters. It is especially necessary to note that in *To the Lighthouse* relationships between characters are as significant as individual personality traits.

MRS RAMSAY

We do not know Mrs Ramsay's first name, so our sense of her is inevitably bound up with her social status as the wife of Mr Ramsay, and mother of eight children. Her duties in those twin roles have closely circumscribed her life's experiences. At the start of the book she is fifty years old, 'her hair grey, her cheek sunk' (p. 6).

She is an imaginative woman; her imagination enables her to feel sympathy for others, but may also be seen to fuel a tendency to exaggerate, an indication perhaps that despite her ostensible acceptance of her lot, she feels, at some level of her being, discontent with the limits set by domestic routine. There is further evidence to support this supposition. For example, she is reputed to have had noble Italian ancestry, and she prefers to regard this romantic background, rather than the more prosaic English and Scottish strands of her family, as the source of her temperament. There are also rumours of a tragic love affair earlier in her life, but on that she remains silent.

The novelist's sister, Vanessa Bell, remarked that in the figure of Mrs Ramsay her sister had effectively brought their mother back to life. She is caring and compassionate but essentially a conservative figure. Although Mrs Ramsay seeks to comfort James, to compensate with kindness for the brutal frankness of her husband and Charles Tansley, she makes no direct challenge to conventionally masculine attitudes. She is concerned to protect her son from his father's insensitivity, but does not act to preclude the likelihood that he will one day become a comparably patriarchal figure. Despite her sense that one of the benefits of being a mother is that 'one's children so often gave one's own perceptions a little thrust forwards' (p. 75), she adheres to the Victorian middle-class values of her own upbringing.

Mrs Ramsay is short-sighted. This physical detail may be read **figuratively** to indicate an attention to matters close at hand, an intimate concern with the details of day-to-day living. It may also register Virginia Woolf's sense that this woman, however admirable, has accepted conventional limitations imposed upon her with a readiness that would be a significant flaw in a younger woman. Cam Ramsay is similarly near-sighted, but there is a sense that her life will be less constrained by conventional limits than her mother's has been.

Mrs Ramsay's compassionate nature makes her alert to the plight of the poor and the suffering, and she desires to help in some practical way to alleviate their distress. In I, 1 she is knitting a stocking for the lighthouse-keeper's son, who is unwell. Her visit to the home of a sick woman in the nearby town is also recalled. She is active in promoting certain improvements in social welfare, which should ameliorate the lot of the underprivileged. But she regards poverty as inevitable. It is, of course, socially determined, but for Mrs Ramsay it seems to have the inexorable quality of a natural law. There is no possibility, within her deeply conservative view of the world, that the social order might be substantially modified to eradicate the causes of poverty.

The process of establishing relationships between people is of paramount importance to her. In fact, drawing people together, overcoming their personal differences, has become her reason for being. Her hospitality is one manifestation of this. She deplores her children's incivility towards guests, even when she might secretly share their view. Her inclination is to assume a maternal role towards men in general: 'Indeed, she had the whole of the other sex under her protection' (p. 5).

In return, she is very sensitive to being liked, and is upset by Mr Carmichael's reserve in the face of her kindness to him. Yet she is also sensitive to the possibility that others might see her kindness as a form of personal vanity. She has been accused of 'Wishing to dominate, wishing to interfere, making people do what she wished' (p. 53). She resents such accusations levelled at her conduct in private relationships, although she admits to being wilful in relation to social welfare concerns such as 'hospitals and drains and the dairy' (p. 53) These concerns are extensions of her maternal role, rather than examples of significant political awareness.

For Mrs Ramsay, marriage is not merely a contract; it is an affirmation of order and stability. Although her life with Mr Ramsay is fraught with tensions, she has faith in marriage above all things, and argues that 'an unmarried woman has missed the best of life' (p. 46). She contrives to bring Paul Rayley and Minta Doyle together, and even hatches plans for a match between Lily Briscoe and William Bankes. But her simple faith in marriage is perceived as a shortcoming by Lily. In practice, the Rayleys' marriage fails. Virginia Woolf seems to be suggesting that although Mrs Ramsay's desire to bring people together harmoniously is admirable, the institution of marriage is not necessarily the most effective means.

Mrs Ramsay loves being a mother, and consequently hates to see her children growing up. Childhood she considers the happiest phase of human life, and she wishes James and Cam could remain at that stage, instead of becoming 'long-legged monsters' (p. 54). She would be happy if always able to have a baby in her arms. Although she is aging physically, she has preserved a sense of fun, and excitedly suggests a visit to the circus.

She is aware of her grey hair and sunken cheeks, but her beauty is regularly noted by other characters. William Bankes regards it as classical beauty: 'The Graces assembling seemed to have joined hands in meadows of asphodel to compose that face.' But that classical perfection is set off by 'some freak of idiosyncrasy' such as incongruous wearing of a deerstalker hat, giving her an air of eccentricity while precluding remoteness from the world around her (p. 27).

Life is described as 'her old antagonist' (p. 74). She struggles against its complexity in order to act as a consoling presence for her family and friends. Although she appears affirmative throughout, she is plagued by fears. Her dedication to order is driven by anxious awareness of the threat of chaos, and her husband recognises her underlying pessimism. Still, she manages to offer 'the relief of simplicity' in a difficult and complicated world (p. 38). Indeed, her directness permits her insight of a kind which her husband, a professional philosopher, cannot emulate: 'Her simplicity fathomed what clever people falsified' (p. 27).

Mr ramsay

The novelist's sister, Vanessa Bell, recognised her father in the character of Mr Ramsay, although she felt this was a lesser accomplishment than the transformation of her mother into Mrs Ramsay, because Leslie Stephen's characteristics lent themselves to such a portrayal.

When his wife first met him the blue-eyed Ramsay was 'gaunt but gallant' (p. 92). At the start of the book, he is described as 'lean as a knife, narrow as the blade of one' (p. 4). This suggests his physical appearance but also his mental acuity, his capacity for abstract analysis. He is described as taking delight in disillusioning his children, in the interests of the truth. Cam sees her father's mind following 'a single narrow path' as he reads (p. 181). In I, 6 the operation of his mind is compared to the letters of the alphabet and the keyboard of a piano. The linearity of his thinking is well suited to logical argument, but it excludes much that forms the field of human experience. Mrs Ramsay has a more encompassing understanding of life.

Mr Ramsay is capable of generating extreme emotional responses in his children. They can feel affection for him, but most often we witness their simmering resentment at his tyrannical presence. He takes pride in respecting facts, however harsh, refusing to falsify, even in order to console his family. His wife, on the other hand, puts consolation before factual accuracy, and that causes discord between husband and wife. Her selfless outlook is often at odds with his egotism. He is a man who demands sympathetic support and requires sacrifices.

Ramsay loves dogs and children; he is essentially kindly. Yet Lily regards him as a 'petty, selfish, vain, egotistical' tyrant, while respecting the fact that he is driven by 'a fiery unworldliness' (p. 23). Mrs Ramsay is struck by her husband's continued physical strength at sixty, and by his intellectual strength which results in optimism, so that 'being convinced, as he was, of all sorts of horrors, seemed not to depress him, but to cheer him' (p. 65). This contrasts with her own underlying pessimism.

At the end of the book he is seventy-one years old. He is regularly presented as a heroic figure, engaged in intellectual adventures that bring him face to face with unpalatable truths. But he is, with equal regularity, regarded as impractical, eccentric, even foolish. Lily Briscoe and William Bankes consider him 'venerable and laughable at one and the same time' (p. 42). His habit of reciting poetry aloud, irrespective of the social context, is a source of embarrassment to others.

He has a mind for extraordinary concepts but tends to be largely oblivious to the ordinary physical world around him. Yet he is concerned with social issues. Mrs Ramsay remarks that her husband cared so much about fishermen and their wages that he lost sleep. He does not participate in her projects, which require personal attention to others, but he does tussle with political ideas and general principles. In doing so, he concludes that the lot of the average person should be of paramount concern in social policy, and he considers art a superficial embellishment, unnecessary in a truly civilised society.

Although he seems to reject art, he avidly reads literature and recites it, and although he seems to endorse the priority of the average, he is obsessed with the nature of greatness, fearing that his own work will not be valued by posterity. In the present there seems to be no shortage of admirers for his intellectual prowess. Charles Tansley is one of numerous young men who regard him as an important mentor. Older friends, such as William Bankes, however, remark that his academic career has suffered as a consequence of demands made by his large family. Bankes believes that Ramsay did his best work before the age of forty. Indeed, he published an important book when twenty-five, and has since then merely repeated and amplified its concerns. Ramsay himself is unsettled by a sense that he might have produced better work had he not married. His wife's passionate advocacy of marriage may be fuelled in part by recognition that her husband is troubled by this suspicion.

CHARLES TANSLEY

Charles Tansley is one of many young men who, out of reverence for his intellect, have sought out Mr Ramsay's company in the remote Hebrides. He is earnest, but a figure of fun amongst the Ramsay children, who know him as 'the little atheist' (p. 5). Physically, they declare him 'a miserable specimen […] all humps and hollows'. Andrew proclaims him 'a sarcastic brute' (p. 6).

Tansley has paid his own way since the age of thirteen. He is one of nine children of a working-class chemist, who derives a modest income from running a shop. His grandfather was a fisherman. He is acutely and uneasily conscious of the class difference separating him from the Ramsays, but he shares with Mr Ramsay a passion for mathematics and philosophy. In the scheme of *To the Lighthouse*, these disciplines are firmly established as masculine domains, more or less closed to women.

Tansley's sensitivity to class distinctions feeds into a potentially explosive cocktail within him:

> He could almost pity these mild cultivated people, who would be blown sky high, like bales of wool and barrels of apples, one of these days by the gunpowder that was in him. (p. 85)

He clearly feels the weight of his class affiliation upon his shoulders as he crosses into the traditional preserve of educated men from the higher classes. The presence in 'Time Passes' of the coarse, gossipy figure of Mrs McNab underlines the cultural and economic distance separating the old working class from the Ramsays, who were in a position to employ servants. Tansley is struggling, tenaciously and with evident bitterness, to cross that divide.

He is presented as a pedantic, unimaginative, and egocentric person, who will turn any topic around until it flatters him and disparages others. Like Mr Ramsay, he regards every conversation as a contest, or a struggle for power, in which he must assert himself. Although he seems to feel genuine respect for Mrs Ramsay, he is convinced of the need for women to subordinate their lives to the requirements of their husbands, who possess more powerful intellects and do the world's real work. He is vocal in his ethical opposition to the First World War, taking a public platform to argue against the government. But his ingrained belief in the social inferiority of women discloses a serious blind spot in his capacity for political analysis.

Towards the end of the novel, Lily remarks that Tansley has been awarded an academic fellowship, has married, and lives at Golder's Green, in North London.

Mr CARMICHAEL

Mr Carmichael is a mysterious, benevolent figure with 'yellow cat's eyes'. He has a 'capacious paunch' (p. 9), and is invariably seen in taciturn, somnolent repose, attributed to opium addiction, which is presumed by the older children to account for canary-yellow staining on his milk-white moustache.

He is a guest, an old friend and former college associate of Mr Ramsay. Carmichael's career as a philosopher, once apparently destined for greatness, ran into difficulties on account of his marriage. This situation has doubtless exacerbated Ramsay's anxiety about the adverse effect of his marriage upon his own career. Carmichael left Oxford for India, and has subsequently experienced financial difficulties.

He lives with his wife in St John's Wood, London. Mrs Ramsay feels that he has been made to suffer countless indignities within the marriage. As a consequence, she feels, he cannot enter into a relationship of trust with her. He composes poetry in his head, as he reclines on the lawn. In 'Time Passes' we learn that he has published a volume of his verse, with some success. Lily Briscoe supposes his verse to be impersonal, but the published volume nonetheless constitutes a bridge out of his narcotic isolation, establishing contact with others. He becomes something of a celebrity, but as Lily observes, he is physically unchanged:

> There was a famous man now called Carmichael, she smiled, thinking how many shapes one person might wear, how he was that in the newspapers, but here the same as he had always been. (p. 185)

Initially, he seems a sad figure, but as the novel unfolds his resources of inner strength and his quiet creativity are revealed. Too old to fight in the war, he is a survivor, who in III, 2 is seen reading a French novel, 'rubicund, drowsy, entirely contented' (p. 145). He is evidently indifferent to worldly success, and has surrendered all ambition in a manner unthinkable to Mr Ramsay. In doing so, he has found peace.

LILY BRISCOE

Lily Briscoe is arguably the most important figure in the novel. She is a woman who refuses to be constrained by the obligations of marriage and parenthood, and a painter who recognises the importance of art as a means of comprehending the world.

Lily is thirty-three years old in 'The Window', forty-four in 'The Lighthouse'. She keeps house for her father, off London's Brompton Road, and feels profound admiration for Mrs Ramsay's capacity to act as a stable centre for her family and social circle. But when Mrs Ramsay argues that an unmarried woman misses out on the best things in life, Lily is filled with resentment. She has an independent spirit, which Mrs Ramsay lacks, and she opts to direct her energies to painting, rather than to the demands of married life.

In contrast to the classically beautiful Mrs Ramsay, Lily appears to lack the conventional attributes of feminine attractiveness. Mrs Ramsay perceives charm in her 'Chinese eyes, aslant in her white, puckered little face' (p. 24), but fears that Lily will never find a husband. She hopes to guide her into a relationship with the widower William Bankes. The couple do become good friends, but Lily is not inclined to marry. Mrs Ramsay's failure to grasp or to take seriously Lily's dedication to painting discloses the limits of her understanding.

Art is Lily's means to emulate Mrs Ramsay in granting coherent form to life's chaotic multiplicity. Importantly for her, as a woman, the creative affirmation of painting allows her to move out from the domestic confines that have constrained her older friend. Virginia Woolf's own decision to become a writer enabled her to experience the world beyond those limits within which her mother, Julia Stephen, led her life. Lily's artistry can be seen as in part a parallel to the novelist's own activity.

The act of painting is a difficult one for her, however, and like Virginia Woolf, she experiences profound anxiety at the heart of her creativity:

> It was in that moment's flight between the picture and her canvas that the demons set on her who often brought her to the verge of tears and made this passage from conception to work as dreadful as any down a dark passage for a child. (pp. 17–18)

She is extremely sensitive about her activity, and dreads the prospect of Mr Ramsay, or anyone else, pausing to look at the painting while it is in progress.

Self-consciousness is an obstacle to be overcome, and eventually she manages to approach her picture 'with all her faculties in a trance, frozen over superficially but moving underneath with extreme speed' (p. 191). She requires a paintbrush in her hand in order to see the scene that she is depicting. It focuses her entire being upon the fulfilment of a particular task, as a pen in a writer's hand might do. That concentration enables her to discern the underlying form which holds the scene together, and that underlying form then becomes the essential element of her picture, the vital ingredient in a successful composition.

WILLIAM BANKES

Bankes, like Lily Briscoe, is staying in rooms in the village, and this helps to establish a bond of friendship between them, even though he has turned sixty and she is only thirty-three. He is a widower with no children. Professionally, he is a botanist, and his scientific interest in flowers contrasts with the artist's aesthetic pleasure in them. He, like Mr Ramsay, manifests conventionally masculine qualities, although he appears notably less self-centred.

Lily considers him finer than Mr Ramsay in his austerity, his isolation and his lack of vanity. At the same time, she is aware that he has brought a valet all the way to Skye, objects to dogs being allowed to occupy chairs, and talks obsessively about the inadequacies of English cooking.

Just as Ramsay is cloistered in his philosophy, so Bankes is 'a man who spent so much time in laboratories that the world when he came out seemed to dazzle him' (p. 168).

Bankes and Ramsay have been close friends, but Bankes is conscious that their meetings are now structured to allow repetition of the familiar, rather than to court new experiences. He expresses the view that his friend's work has been impeded by the demands of family life. Lily draws confirmation from this for her own view of marriage and parenthood. In light of this, it appears **ironic** that Mrs Ramsay should harbour hopes that the couple might marry.

MINTA DOYLE AND PAUL RAYLEY

Mrs Ramsay sees Minta Doyle as a tomboy, perhaps because the twenty-four-year-old woman has not yet settled into conventional gender roles. Certainly, Minta behaves in a boisterous fashion, which leads Andrew to admire her reckless spirit. Her ebullience is reflected in her singing of popular songs. Initially, she appears fearless with a taste for adventure, but her conventionally feminine vulnerability is soon disclosed, and she readily agrees to become Paul Rayley's wife.

Paul Rayley is a young man for whom the proposal to Minta is a major step into the responsibilities of maturity. But he is uneasy at the prospect of marriage, and it appears that Mrs Ramsay's prompting to make the proposal was premature. This is borne out in the unsatisfactory course of the couple's married life. We are told that he occupied himself breeding Belgian hares, and playing chess in coffee houses. Then the Rayleys fell out of love, and Paul took a mistress.

THE RAMSAY CHILDREN

The Ramsays have eight children. The youngest, James and Cam, feature most prominently in the novel, being the focus of their mother's attention in 'The Window', and accompanying their father on the trip to the Lighthouse in the final part of the book.

William Bankes dubs the little boy James the Ruthless. His mother, on the other hand, considers him the most sensitive of her children. He continues as a teenager to resent his father's tyrannical behaviour, but there are clear indications in 'The Lighthouse' that James will soon feel at home with the conventional masculine values that his father embodies. The symbolism of the novel prepares us for this assimilation: when we first encounter James, he is wielding scissors, cutting out pictures. Blade imagery is associated throughout with the analytical masculine mind.

Bankes considers Cam 'wild and fierce' (p. 20). Her imagination is such that she can transform the trip to the Lighthouse into a much more exotic adventure, 'a great expedition'. When her father proffers her a gingerbread nut, he seems 'a great Spanish gentleman, she thought, handing a flower to a lady at a window' (p. 195). She inherits that imaginative capacity from her mother, but Cam remains unconstrained by responsibilities. It appears that she will be able to live, as a member of a younger generation, more adventurously than her mother.

Bankes recognises Andrew's intelligence; he is a good mathematician, and Mr Ramsay envisages him succeeding in an academic career. But he is killed by a shell during the First World War. Virginia Woolf presents him as a young man of promise sacrificed to the ethical bankruptcy of the patriarchal order.

Prue inherits her mother's beauty; Bankes thinks of her as Prue the Fair (p. 21). She marries, but dies of illness associated with childbirth. She has followed Mrs Ramsay's path, accepting the roles of wife and mother. But it does not work out, as if to suggest that the example of domesticity carries inadequate weight following the traumas of the First World War. Mrs Ramsay's day has passed. Virginia Woolf saw art as the vital corrective to the formlessness of modern life, so Lily Briscoe, rather than Prue, is the key figure.

Little is said of Roger, although his wildness as a child is noted. Jasper shoots at birds. His father considers it natural for a boy to display

CHARACTERISATION continued

aggression. His mother disapproves, but accepts that it is a stage he is going through. We are told that 'he shared his mother's vice: he, too, exaggerated' (p. 74).

Rose is gifted manually, making dresses, arranging flowers, and so on. She helps her mother choose jewellery and Mrs Ramsay sees her as a girl with deep feelings. Still, their mother perceives in the older Ramsay girls rebelliousness against that traditional domestic order in which she remains immersed. They manifest desire for greater personal freedom, even, in the case of Nancy, for a wild life.

THEMES

GENDER

Virginia Woolf sustains a tension between public and private, home and the outside world, throughout the novel. Following the fashion of middle-class Victorian England, the world in which her own parents had grown up, she identifies the domestic sphere with women and conventionally feminine values, and the public world with men and conventionally masculine values. Virginia Woolf is schematic in the way she sustains this division, but her intention is ultimately critical of its authority.

Mr Ramsay believes that gendered behaviour is governed by the laws of nature. He argues that Jasper shoots at birds because he is a boy. A peculiarity of one woman becomes an illustration of how women necessarily act. Virginia Woolf saw that behavioural patterns were deeply engrained, but she also recognised the part played by training in forming gendered attitudes and setting horizons of expectation.

Mrs Ramsay embodies conventional domestic virtues, and she respects the cultural dominance of masculine intelligence, which she conceives 'like iron girders spanning the swaying fabric, upholding the world, so that she could trust herself to it utterly' (p. 98). But for Virginia Woolf that structure collapsed amid the carnage of the First World War, and she presents Lily Briscoe's dedication to art as a potential means to bridge the damaging divide between masculine and feminine values.

Although she came from a relatively privileged background, Virginia Woolf was not granted the university education her brothers received, because she was a woman. The resistance she experienced to the notion of women creating art is reflected in Charles Tansley's bigoted remarks concerning the inability of women to paint or write.

SOCIAL CRITICISM

The emphasis that Virginia Woolf placed upon the importance of art should not be mistaken for indifference to pressing social issues. Art for her, as for many of her contemporaries in writing, painting and music, had a vital role to play in the wake of the First World War. She felt that the war was a graphic demonstration of the ethical bankruptcy of the prevailing patriarchal order, which privileged conventionally masculine values and scientific understanding. Her work during the 1920s consistently challenged those values and that understanding, and argued for promotion of feminine values and of the insights gained through art.

Mr Ramsay, the embodiment of the patriarchy, seems harmless enough, despite his eccentricities and his egotism. But the death of his son Andrew, fighting in France is offered in 'Time Passes' as one of those stark facts that Ramsay cherishes. It is evidently an appalling waste of human potential. In Virginia Woolf's view the structure of values that Ramsay represents underpins such horrors. So her social criticism crucially involves reassessment of conventional gender roles, according to which men belong to the public world of practical collective action, while women merely fulfil domestic duties. She schematises this distinction in such a way that the public world appears cut off from personal sensations and emotions. The world beyond the home appears desensitised. It is a world in which young men are sent to die in large numbers. Virginia Woolf sought through her art to help restore collective value based on awareness of the value of individual experience, in all its complexity.

SUBJECT AND OBJECT AND THE NATURE OF REALITY

Andrew Ramsay sums up his father's philosophical work in the phrase 'Subject and object and the nature of reality' (p. 21). These are weighty philosophical concerns, but they are also issues addressed exhaustively in Virginia Woolf's novel. She felt that philosophical models, although they might appear coherent, invariably violate the wholeness of existence. The fabric of living was shredded by the analytical edge of philosophical argument. Art, she believed, could elucidate the relationship of the self to the world beyond the self, while preserving the integrity of lived experience. This is Lily Briscoe's aspiration.

Virginia Woolf also sought to achieve this elucidation, but note that throughout the novel there is reference to the inadequacy of language to convey accurately what it is to be alive. As Lily observes, 'Little words that broke up the thought and dismembered it said nothing', and she asks 'how could one express in words these emotions of the body?' (p. 169). Nonetheless, Virginia Woolf chose words as the medium of her art. In place of the discrete characters of conventional **realist fiction**, she managed to weave a continuous fabric, moving between separate consciousnesses, and out into the world beyond. Her fluid narrative voice was developed in order to handle 'Subject and object and the nature of reality' in a synthetic rather than an analytical way, drawing all together rather than holding elements apart.

Virginia Woolf draws our attention to being, to the life of the world, as well as to individual lives. Mr Ramsay is egotistical in a characteristically patriarchal fashion, but Virginia Woolf reminds us that while individuals inevitably die, being continues, pulsing through the processes of the natural world as well as through human existence.

TIME

'Time Passes' declares the title of the middle section of the novel. But Virginia Woolf recognised that the passage of time is a complex phenomenon, which we can conceive in a variety of ways. Reading *To the Lighthouse* involves a singular rhythm on account of the irregular length of the three parts, and of the smaller sections that comprise them. Sentences also vary dramatically in length, from terse statements to labyrinthine structures involving numerous subordinate clauses. The pace of reading varies.

The novel's content also is concerned with the fluid and elastic nature of our experience of time. The clock-face and the calendar impose regularity, with time divided into seconds, minutes, hours, weeks, months and years. But chronometry tells us little about our lived experience of time passing. Boredom or discomfort can make a brief period seem inordinately long. Intense pleasure can make a longer time seem fleeting, or we may, like Mrs Ramsay at her dinner party, feel we have experienced eternity.

The first, long part of the novel occupies a day. The final part also focuses upon a single day. The brief middle part covers ten years. 'Time Passes' reflects the rhythmical cycle of natural processes, following a fundamental temporal pattern, indifferent to human concerns. This part of the novel intersects with time as recorded in history, the period of the First World War. Historical record also is largely indifferent to the course of individual lives. Historians discuss battles and governmental decisions. It requires a novelist like Virginia Woolf to tell us of the death of Andrew Ramsay, enabling us to sense the depth of loss in the life of his family.

Another important aspect of the treatment of time in the novel is Virginia Woolf's concern with memory. The children live more intensely in the here and now, but for the adults the past forms a kind of filter through which they read the present. Remembering incidents shapes their response to current circumstances. Like the great French novelist Marcel Proust (1871–1922), Virginia Woolf was fascinated by involuntary memory, where some association, often obscure, conjures up recollection of an event long past. This phenomenon suggests that all individual experience is stored somewhere in the mind, awaiting the stimulus that will draw it to the surface. It is often trivial, apparently incidental details that trigger the memory, acquiring more profound significance in the process.

DESIRE

Memory features extensively in the novel, but anticipation is an equally important element. Characters are seen anticipating some future event, which usually reveals their private desires. James desires to visit the Lighthouse, which represents for him unfamiliar experience and the excitement of the unknown. Mrs Ramsay's desire to visit the circus may be seen as a parallel to her son's desire to visit the Lighthouse; it promises a departure from routine. Later we see her envisaging herself in Rome and in India, then Cam imagines the exotic city of Constantinople, and like Lily desires adventures from which women are conventionally excluded. For Lily and Cam, such desiring seems to have a subversive effect, undermining their capacity to feel content with familiar horizons and domestic responsibilities.

ART

Mr Ramsay, musing on the basic requirements for a civilised society, concludes that art is an unnecessary embellishment. Mrs Ramsay, although interested in Lily Briscoe, shows no real interest in her painting. William Bankes, a scientist, shows interest but does not understand what she is doing. Charles Tansley merely remarks that women cannot paint or write.

Lily is arguably the most important character in *To the Lighthouse*, not on account of any distinctive personal characteristic, such as beauty or intelligence, but because of her dedication to art as an affirmation of form and of order in a potentially formless and chaotic world. The waning of religious belief amongst intellectuals led many of Virginia Woolf's contemporaries to look to art for the sense of unity and meaning in life that religion had long supplied. The Irish novelist James Joyce (1882–1941) saw himself as a kind of secular priest. Virginia Woolf was less portentous. It is Mrs Ramsay who provides Lily with her crucial example, although the older woman acts within a domestic context, which Virginia Woolf considered inadequate, especially in the years following the First World War. Importantly, Lily is a woman as well as an artist, and Virginia Woolf's feminism was essentially concerned with women's ability to make significant contributions to cultural life.

LANGUAGE & STYLE

At first encounter, *To the Lighthouse* seems a difficult novel to read. It is Virginia Woolf's innovative narrative technique that initially poses a challenge. Her vocabulary is straightforward. Her style is distinctive (an isolated passage written by Virginia Woolf is easily identified as her work), but once you are familiar with it, it is easily comprehended. There are some features that merit particular note.

VARIABLE SENTENCE LENGTH

Virginia Woolf's sentences are strikingly variable in length. Some are brief and direct. Others are long and immensely complex, incorporating a series of subordinate clauses. This variation contributes to the novel's distinctively irregular rhythmic structure. It also reflects Virginia Woolf's concern with the irregularity of our experience of time, which appears at odds with the regular intervals measured by clocks. Generally (although not invariably), the short sentences make simple statements about objects or events, while the longer sentences reflect the presence of those objects or events within the consciousness of an onlooker. Virginia Woolf uses this difference in order to show the limitations of Mr Ramsay's faith in simple facts (see Textual Analysis – Text 1).

REPETITIVENESS

Phrases, words, and images tend to recur throughout *To the Lighthouse*. Patterns of repetition are characteristic of Virginia Woolf's style. They serve, technically, to help hold the materials of the fiction together, in the absence of a strong storyline. They also assist characterisation, with repetition often indicating an obsession that is constant amid that changeability which is the most striking aspect of Virginia Woolf's approach to character. Such repetition additionally traces the working of memory, as it draws past experiences into the present.

Repetition affirms an underlying regularity beneath the changeable and fragmented surface of life. Lily recognises this constancy:

> For in the rough and tumble of daily life, with all those children about, all those visitors, one had constantly a sense of repetition – of one thing falling where another had fallen, and so setting up an echo which chimed in the air and made it full of vibrations. (p. 189)

Virginia Woolf's style embraces variability, but it also incorporates repetition.

FIGURATIVE LANGUAGE

Virginia Woolf uses striking **similes** that stand out from the flow of her prose. So Mrs Ramsay's courtesy is described as being 'like a Queen's raising from the mud a beggar's dirty foot and washing' (p. 6). Mr Ramsay retreating into the garden from the drawing-room window is said to be like 'the great sea lion at the Zoo tumbling backwards after swallowing his fish and walloping off so that the water in the tank washes from side to side' (p. 30). The latter example illustrates the power of Mrs Ramsay's imagination, as the thought is attributed to her.

More generally, such **figurative language** displays an imaginative capacity to draw disparate entities into unexpected relationships. Such drawing together is, of course, Mrs Ramsay's strength, but Virginia Woolf regarded it as a fundamental activity of the artist. It casts light upon an experience not by the analytical process of dissecting it, but by the synthetic process of combining it with another experience. Mr Ramsay's mind plodding along a straight line would not be capable of the illumination that results from such bold leaps.

SYMBOLISM

Virginia Woolf makes bold use of **symbols**. This basically means that certain images, or groups of images recur, and meanings or associations cluster around them. An obvious example is the group of blade images, which appear in both literal and figurative contexts. We see James using scissors; his father is compared to a knife and a scimitar. The blades come to symbolise a conventionally masculine capacity for incisive analysis. They stand for a particular kind of intelligence, while also suggesting an attitude of aggression.

Waves assume **symbolic** significance as they literally beat against the shore of the island. They embody the concept of continuity and stability underlying surface turbulence and fragmentation. Amid the waves stands the Lighthouse, a symbol of the isolation that threatens all individual lives, but also an object of consciousness, casting symbolic light upon the crucial question of 'Subject, object, and the nature of reality'.

To the Lighthouse is divided into three main parts. These in turn are divided into smaller, numbered sections, which vary markedly in length. The irregular length of these sections constitutes a distinctive structural rhythm. Virginia Woolf is not regulating her narrative divisions mechanically, like clockwork. Rather, she seems to be reflecting the irregularity of our experience of events. Some sections are extended; some are extremely compact. Her form is elastic and flexible, as it must be to accommodate her fluent narrative and complex characterisation.

Stream of consciousness

Despite the structural divisions, Virginia Woolf's narrative voice remains remarkably fluent. It is ostensibly a third-person narration, yet the voice moves freely from the consciousness of one character to that of another. It also engages directly with events in the exterior world. Virginia Woolf avoids granting her narrative voice a distinct identity. It is not linked to a particular person, and its flexible nature does not suggest any single type of person. It can be seen as a sophisticated development of the **free indirect style** evolved by earlier novelists such as Jane Austen (1775–1817).

Virginia Woolf's technique is often referred to as **stream of consciousness**, a term derived from the American psychologist William James (1842–1910). A major contribution to that technique was made by Virginia Woolf's contemporary Dorothy Richardson (1873–1957) in her novel sequence *Pilgrimage* (1915–38). Stream of consciousness, which Virginia Woolf employs with singular skill, allows her to explore the nature of individual perception in relationship to collective understanding.

Point of view

The term **stream of consciousness** is sometimes applied to writing that presents the contents of only a single character's mind. Virginia Woolf's narration is more ambitious and more subtle than that kind of **interior monologue**. It was crucial to her purpose that the thought processes of several characters should be shown. This allowed her to demonstrate the importance of point of view. A single event can be witnessed simultaneously by two or more characters, who then interpret it in differing ways. The differences may be trivial, or they may be considerable. Such divergences assist characterisation, enabling us to evaluate a character according to their response.

In Virginia Woolf's fictional world, changing circumstances, even slight variations of mood or situation, can produce a modified interpretation from each point of view. Once we recognise that reality consists not of simple objects and unequivocal events, but of multiple perspectives and contesting interpretations, the faith in facts preserved by Mr Ramsay appears untenable, and we can appreciate what his wife has accomplished in drawing all together (even momentarily).

Virginia Woolf insists on the difficulty of gauging what another person feels at any particular moment. Lily Briscoe, watching Mrs Ramsay, expresses the daunting prospect faced by all who try to grasp another person's point of view: 'One wanted fifty pairs of eyes to see with, she reflected. Fifty pairs of eyes were not enough to get round that one woman with, she thought.' She continues:

> One wanted most some secret sense, fine as air, with which to steal through keyholes and surround her where she sat knitting, talking, sitting silent in the window alone; which took to itself and treasured up like the air which held the smoke of the steamer, her thoughts, her imaginations, her desires. What did the hedge mean to her, what did the garden mean to her, what did it mean to her when a wave broke? (p. 188)

ATTENTION TO DETAIL

A striking feature of Virginia Woolf's writing is her close attention to details that may appear trivial or irrelevant. Other novelists, with conventionally masculine sensibilities, have composed panoramic sweeps, taking in whole societies and entire historical epochs. Virginia Woolf felt it was important, especially in the aftermath of the First World War, to attend to the intimate details that comprise individual existence. Panoramic sweeps require abstraction, which results in omission of the real substance of life. Virginia Woolf preferred to work with the fabric of everyday life, made up of countless sensations, insignificant actions and customarily unrecorded occurrences. There, she felt, real human value might be found.

MOTIFS

In looking at Virginia Woolf's style we noted her use of **symbols**. From a technical point of view, these images may be regarded as **motifs**, recurrent elements that help to bind the prose, and to assist our understanding as we read. Because she is not telling a story in a conventional sense, recurrent images, words and phrases help to hold the fictional composition together, like co-ordinate points marked on a map. These motifs are examples of Virginia Woolf's calculated use of repetition. In Lily Briscoe's evocative terms, they constitute 'one thing falling where another had fallen, and so setting up an echo which chimed in the air and made it full of vibrations' (p. 189).

PARENTHETICAL REMARKS

Virginia Woolf's narrative voice is extraordinarily fluent, especially given its frequent shifts of viewpoint. One of the techniques she employs to preserve this fluency is to place potentially disruptive remarks inside brackets. These remarks often function like asides in a play, supplying commentary upon the thoughts or actions in which they are embedded. They can also create a sort of counterpoint between one level of activity and another. So, in I, 11 Mrs Ramsay's meditation is played against her knitting: 'Not as oneself did one find rest ever, in her experience (she accomplished here something dexterous with her needles), but as a wedge of darkness' (p. 58). The use of brackets allows thought and action to be shown occurring simultaneously. It enables Virginia Woolf to reflect the unremittingly continuous nature of reality, in which there are always many things taking place at once.

The most dramatic use of **parentheses** is to be found in 'Time Passes'. Here, characters we have come to know in the first part of the novel are consigned to terse, matter-of-fact parenthetical statements, contained in square brackets at the end of each section. These serve to shift the focus of our attention from the experiences of individual lives to the fundamental processes of being, from isolated lives to the life of the world.

FLASHBACKS

Memory is an important thematic concern of this novel. Characters'
recollections usually occur fleetingly, in the course of more general
thought processes. But occasionally, Virginia Woolf uses a **flashback**
technique which reconstructs the events that occasioned a particular
memory as if they were unfolding in the present. In the opening section
of 'The Window', Mrs Ramsay recalls a walk to the nearby town
accompanied by Charles Tansley. As we read the account it does not
appear to be contained within Mrs Ramsay's consciousness. Rather,
it is recounted by the narrative voice, exercising its remarkable capacity
to shift to another point of view through time, as well as through space.
It seems for a while that the walk is taking place in present time, but
the start of I, 2 jolts us back to the narrative's actual present, where
Mrs Ramsay remains in the drawing room with her son, James.

Part four

Textual analysis

TEXT 1 (I, 6 PAGES 31–2)

He was safe, he was restored to his privacy. He stopped to light his pipe, looked once at his wife and son in the window, and as one raises one's eyes from a page in an express train and sees a farm, a tree, a cluster of cottages as an illustration, a confirmation of something on the printed page to which one returns, fortified, and satisfied, so without his distinguishing either his son or his wife, the sight of them fortified him and satisfied him and consecrated his effort to arrive at a perfectly clear understanding of the problem which now engaged the energies of his splendid mind.

It was a splendid mind. For if thought is like the keyboard of a piano, divided into so many notes, or like the alphabet is ranged in twenty-six letters all in order, then his splendid mind had no sort of difficulty in running over those letters one by one, firmly and accurately, until it had reached, say, the letter Q. He reached Q. Very few people in the whole of England ever reach Q. Here, stopping for one moment by the stone urn which held the geraniums, he saw, but now far far away, like children picking up shells, divinely innocent and occupied with little trifles at their feet and somehow entirely defenceless against a doom which he perceived, his wife and son, together, in the window. They needed his protection; he gave it them. But after Q? What comes next? After Q there are a number of letters the last of which is scarcely visible to mortal eyes, but glimmers red in the distance. Z is only reached once by one man in a generation. Still, if he could reach R it would be something. Here at least was Q. He dug his heels in at Q. Q he was sure of. Q he could demonstrate. If Q then is Q – R – Here he knocked his pipe out, with two or three resonant taps on the ram's horn which made the handle of the urn, and proceeded. 'Then R ...' He braced himself. He clenched himself.

Qualities that would have saved a ship's company exposed on a broiling sea with six biscuits and a flask of water – endurance and justice, foresight, devotion, skill, came to his help. R is then – what is R?

A shutter, like the leathern eyelid of a lizard, flickered over the intensity of his gaze and obscured the letter R. In that flash of darkness he heard people saying –

he was a failure – that R was beyond him. He would never reach R. On to R, once more. R–

Qualities that in a desolate expedition across the icy solitudes of the Polar region would have made him the leader, the guide, the counsellor, whose temper, neither sanguine nor despondent, surveys with equanimity what is to be and faces it, came to his help again. R–

The lizard's eye flickered once more. The veins on his forehead bulged. The geranium in the urn became startlingly visible and, displayed among its leaves, he could see, without wishing it, that old, that obvious distinction between the two classes of men; on the one hand the steady goers of superhuman strength who, plodding and persevering, repeat the whole alphabet in order, twenty-six letters in all, from start to finish; on the other the gifted, the inspired who, miraculously, lump all the letters together in one flash – the way of genius.

Mrs Ramsay, throughout the first part of the novel, endeavours to draw people together. Here, on the other hand, we see Mr Ramsay seeking the isolation that will allow him to pursue his philosophical work. He is a man whose professional life is conducted in public, yet he requires privacy to develop ideas. Perhaps we can compare him to the Lighthouse, physically separated, but casting light to guide others. Less charitably, we can see his desire for privacy as a manifestation of his egotism, a form of selfishness which often generates resentment amongst those who know him, including his own children.

'The Window' is the title of this part of the book. It refers to the transparent surface where interior and exterior meet. In **figurative** terms, a window may be said to represent the point of contact between subject and object. The relationship between the two is a primary concern of this novel (see Theme on Subject, Object, and the Nature of Reality).

Lily Briscoe, throughout the first sections of the novel, paints Mrs Ramsay and James, framed by the window. Ramsay also derives satisfaction from seeing his wife and son within that frame. Note, however, that his satisfaction is compared to the experience of a traveller, looking out and finding that the exterior world corresponds to something asserted in a book. The printed page carries authority for Ramsay; he is inclined to trust it above any evidence non-verbal reality supplies. Reason carries greater authority for him than sensory experience. Compare the

moment in 'The Lighthouse' where Lily Briscoe is said to resemble a
traveller, who:

> even though he is half asleep, knows, looking out of the train window, that he
> must look now, for he will never see that town, or that mule-cart, or that woman
> at work in the fields, again. (p. 184)

For her, the unique sensation of being in the world is paramount.

Mr Ramsay has the mind of a professional philosopher. It is
compared to the arrangement of notes on a piano keyboard, and of letters
in the alphabet. Virginia Woolf uses the word 'if'; it is clear from the
nature of her work that she did not believe that 'thought is like the
keyboard of a piano'. In an essay entitled 'Modern Fiction', written in
1919, she argued that 'life is not a series of gig lamps symmetrically
arranged'. Rather, it is 'a luminous halo, a semi-transparent envelope
surrounding us from the beginning of consciousness to the end'. In
Virginia Woolf's understanding, reality is a complex and continuous field
of simultaneous experiences, not a straight line formed from units
arranged in logical sequence.

The linear bias of Ramsay's thinking may explain his fondness for
Alfred, Lord Tennyson's poem 'The Charge of the Light Brigade'. It
celebrates soldiers who rode straight to their deaths, with cannon to both
right and left. Tennyson sees glory in their single-mindedness, but
Virginia Woolf was writing a decade after the terrible battle of the
Somme in which many thousands of men were slaughtered in rapid
succession as they advanced towards the enemy. She knew that modern
warfare was inglorious. She also felt that the blinkered linearity of
patriarchal thinking lay behind the slaughter.

Pursuing her **simile** of the alphabet, Virginia Woolf declares that
Ramsay has reached Q. It seems significant that Q precedes R, the first
letter of his own name. The implication might be that he lacks self-
knowledge, for all his cleverness and his egotism. But Ramsay is sure of
'Q'. He can feel confident of his understanding at that point on the line.
'Q.E.D.' is an abbreviation often placed at the end of mathematical or
scientific proofs. It stands for *quod erat demonstrandum*, a Latin phrase
meaning 'which was to be proved'. A verbal echo occurs in the statement
'Q he could demonstrate' suggesting a deliberate evocation, which
consolidates association of Ramsay with printed scientific proofs.

Z, the end of the line, the conclusion of the quest 'is only reached once by one man in a generation'. The gendered nature of this statement is not incidental. The analytical mind conventionally associated with masculine thinking may struggle towards 'Z', and it may take a special individual to reach it, but Virginia Woolf seems to suggest that with her capacity for synthesis Mrs Ramsay is able to encompass the entire alphabet, at once (see Textual Analysis – Text 2). Women may intuitively achieve the result that men strive vainly to attain through reasoning.

The sentence starting 'Here, stopping for one moment by the stone urn ...' has a complex structure, incorporating subordinate clauses, which runs counter to the linear conception of Ramsay's thought process suggested by analogy with the alphabet or a piano keyboard. It is a sentence that seems to fold in on itself, not just a simple statement of fact, but a knot of relationships. Virginia Woolf's prose mirrors the complexity of the world, casting an **ironic** light on the line pursued by Ramsay's analytical mind.

The ram's horn on which Ramsay knocks his pipe may be brought to mind in reading I, 18, where Cam is frightened by a boar's skull, complete with tusks, which hangs upon her bedroom wall. There are in this novel a number of comparable **symbols** associated with masculine aggression. Significantly, James enjoys the sight of the skull on the wall (see Contemporary Approaches – Freudian Criticism).

The narrative voice suggests that Mr Ramsay's struggle with a philosophical problem requires all the resourcefulness of a sea-captain saving lives in a crisis. He is also compared to an intrepid polar explorer. Making gentle fun of Mr Ramsay, Virginia Woolf is **parodying** conventional masculine attributes as they appear in tales of adventure. Adventure has traditionally been undertaken by men, and when, later in the novel, both Lily Briscoe and Cam Ramsay crave the experience, we are reminded that women have generally been excluded from it. In 'The Lighthouse', Mr Ramsay, who is prone to self-dramatisation, regards himself as a heroic adventurer, even though the voyage takes him only a short distance from the shore. The philosopher, sixty years old here, seventy-one in the final part, appears incongruous in the context of physical action, but we might discern an element of heroic determination in his pursuit of intellectual adventure.

The image of a shutter covering Ramsay's gaze seems to support a parallel at this point between this solitary man and the Lighthouse, whose beam is interrupted at regular intervals by means of a shutter. The phrase 'flash of darkness' is paradoxical, but consolidates evocation of the Lighthouse. Virginia Woolf employs a characteristically striking **simile**, evoking the eyelid of a lizard, with the archaic adjective 'leathern' suggesting its texture more effectively than the more familiar 'leathery'. The image is used **figuratively** to identify a moment of insecurity, in which Ramsay is troubled by a sense of professional failure. Such doubts recur in the novel, and are often linked to a suspicion that marriage and parenthood, the twin pillars of his wife's existence, have diminished his contribution to philosophy. Tension exists between husband and wife on account of this sense that his family commitments have compromised Ramsay's public status.

Virginia Woolf, always intensely interested in the workings of consciousness, also isolates telling details of physical appearance. She moves into close-up, to use a cinematographic analogy, in order to show how 'The veins on his forehead bulged', an external indication of the intensity of his thought processes. The narrative voice then adopts his point of view to stress his concentrated attention upon the geranium in its urn. Mr Ramsay's abstract classification of men is said to take form within the plant's leaves. Virginia Woolf seems to be pointing out that abstract thought is actually embedded in the physical reality of the world, to which Mr Ramsay belongs despite his rarefied mind. Remember that in I, 4 we are told that whenever Lily Briscoe thought of Mr Ramsay's work 'she always saw clearly before her a large kitchen table' (p. 21).

Virginia Woolf's essay, 'Modern Fiction', can be found in her book *The Common Reader* (Hogarth Press, 1925; Penguin Books, 1992).

TEXT 2   (I, 11 PAGES 57–8)

> She could be herself, by herself. And that was what now she often felt the need of
> – to think; well not even to think. To be silent; to be alone. All the being and the
> doing, expansive, glittering, vocal, evaporated; and one shrunk, with a sense of
> solemnity, to being oneself, a wedge-shaped core of darkness, something invisible
> to others. Although she continued to knit, and sat upright, it was thus that she felt

herself; and this self having shed its attachments was free for the strangest adventures. When life sank down for a moment, the range of experience seemed limitless. And to everybody there was always this sense of unlimited resources, she supposed; one after another, she, Lily, Augustus Carmichael, must feel, our apparitions, the things you know us by, are simply childish. Beneath it is all dark, it is all spreading, it is unfathomably deep; but now and again we rise to the surface and that is what you see us by. Her horizon seemed to her limitless. There were all the places she had not seen; the Indian plains; she felt herself pushing aside the thick leather curtain of a church in Rome. This core of darkness could go anywhere, for no one saw it. They could not stop it, she thought, exulting. There was freedom, there was peace, there was, most welcome of all, a summoning together, a resting on a platform of stability. Not as oneself did one find rest ever, in her experience (she accomplished here something dexterous with her needles), but as a wedge of darkness. Losing personality, one lost the fret, the hurry, the stir; and there rose to her lips always some exclamation of triumph over life when things came together in this peace, this rest, this eternity; and pausing there she looked out to meet that stroke of the Lighthouse, the long steady stroke, the last of the three, which was her stroke, for watching them in this mood always at this hour one could not help attaching oneself to one thing especially of the things one saw; and this thing, the long steady stroke, was her stroke. Often she found herself sitting and looking, sitting and looking, with her work in her hands until she became the thing she looked at – that light for example. And it would lift up on it some little phrase or other which had been lying in her mind like that – 'Children don't forget, children don't forget' – which she would repeat and begin adding to it, It will end, It will end, she said. It will come, it will come, when suddenly she added, We are in the hands of the Lord.

But instantly she was annoyed with herself for saying that. Who had said it? not she; she had been trapped into saying something she did not mean. She looked up over her knitting and met the third stroke and it seemed to her like her own eyes meeting her own eyes, searching as she alone could search into her mind and heart, purifying out of her existence that lie, any lie. She praised herself in praising the light, without vanity, for she was stern, she was searching, she was beautiful like that light.

For most of this first part of the novel, Mrs Ramsay is characteristically engaged in some form of social activity. We see her supporting her husband, looking after her children, matchmaking, attending to guests, visiting a sick woman and overseeing a dinner party. But in this passage she is alone, and she has the opportunity to 'be herself'. Our sense of Mrs Ramsay's self is comprehensively bound up with her social role as wife and mother. Her identity seems to be bonded to the conventions of marital life and to the routine activities of parenthood, so it is revelatory to find that she is aware of the constraints she has chosen to live within, and is able at times like this to detach herself from them.

Mr Ramsay has a strong sense of what constitutes the natural behaviour of women. He mistakes deeply engrained social convention for nature's law. His wife here moves beyond that social convention and experiences what it is like to be in the world, without obligations or responsibilities. In effect she sheds the social identity that is concentrated in the name 'Mrs Ramsay'. The label is removed, and she recognises herself embodied in 'a wedge-shaped core of darkness'.

This **metaphor** is used to identify her essential being, which underlies the socially recognised self. We might call this part of her 'being alive' or 'existing'. It is what a human being has in common with all other animate life. This 'core of darkness' lies beyond language and beyond thought. It is more fundamental than the self as it is known socially, or even as it is known within an individual's self-consciousness.

Mrs Ramsay continues to knit, but at the same time she experiences this profound encounter with her fundamental nature. On the surface she is in motion, underneath there is stability. This dual aspect may recall the image of the waves, which occurs regularly throughout the novel, and which also combines surface agitation with underlying wholeness. The 'wedge of darkness' participates in 'a summoning together, a resting on a platform of stability', the attainment of which is Mrs Ramsay's goal throughout her life.

In the depths of her being she finds freedom not allowed her in daily life. Shedding her social role she also sheds the constraints that delimit her experience as a woman. The term 'adventure' recurs in *To the Lighthouse* indicating conventionally masculine exploits. Lily Briscoe and Cam both desire adventure, while Mr Ramsay's qualities are compared to those of a sea-captain and a polar explorer (see Textual Analysis – Text 1). Here, Mrs Ramsay finds herself free for 'the strangest adventures'. Her imagination, usually hemmed in by her responsibilities, becomes uninhibited and unrestrained, and her world appears 'limitless'.

She imagines herself in places she has not seen: Italy, where some of her ancestors resided; India, a part of the British Empire where her uncle had spent time.

She refers to social selves as 'apparitions', suggesting that our knowledge of one another on a day-to-day basis is illusory. Beneath this politely conventional surface lie 'unlimited resources', the vast potential of imagination and of the basic energy required for being alive. She is intensely aware of the limits in routine existence. Mrs Ramsay has not only accepted the domestic confinement of marriage and parenthood, she actively advocates it for other women. But her vision of total freedom necessarily involves full recognition of the barriers imposed upon her by conventional requirements and expectations.

It is clear that Mrs Ramsay considers life to be a continual struggle to establish order against the forces of chaos. Here she experiences a sense of triumph in that struggle, and feels connected to eternity. Significantly, she has a comparably triumphant moment, with an intimation of eternity during her dinner party in I, 17. Here we see her in isolation, shedding her social self; there she is at the heart of a gathering, immersed in her role as hostess. At both extremes she attains momentarily her ideal of order and stability.

Mrs Ramsay's communion with the Lighthouse beam appears to show how the distinction of subject and object, self and other, may be temporarily resolved. The bridging of that gap, which so preoccupies her husband's philosophical mind, is a vital element in her triumph: 'she became the thing she looked at'. The sense of resolution is made stronger for us because the 'wedge of darkness' which is her essential nature may be seen to match and merge with the wedge-shaped beam of light that issues from the Lighthouse. Although 'she praised herself in praising the light' she did so 'without vanity'. Compare this to her husband's relentless egotism.

A good example of Virginia Woolf's use of **parenthetical** comment occurs in this passage. The observation '(she accomplished here something dexterous with her needles)' reminds us that Mrs Ramsay continues to knit, drawing together physically, as she experiences 'a summoning together' in the depths of her being. The use of brackets enables Virginia Woolf to convey events occurring at different levels simultaneously.

The phrase, 'children don't forget', reminds us of the importance of memory in this novel. Virginia Woolf was fascinated by the involuntary occurrence of memory, so things ostensibly long forgotten emerge from the depths of the mind as a result of some obscure association. Such uninvited recollection implies that all our experiences are stored away somewhere within the self, awaiting the prompt that will summon them back to consciousness (see Theme on Time).

The thought of her children growing older leads Mrs Ramsay to contemplate the inevitability of death ('It will come, it will come'). Her thoughts turn to the beneficent God of Christian belief, perhaps recalled from her own childhood's pious observance. But immediately she recants her piety, for she has evidently lost her faith. Mrs Ramsay may be seen as the embodiment of an epoch in this shift from mid-Victorian orthodox belief to early twentieth-century rejection of Christianity as a 'lie' (see Historical Background – Contemporary Pessimism). Remember that she has lived amongst philosophers and scientists who are undoubtedly sceptics in religion. Her children, evidently raised nonetheless as believers, call Charles Tansley 'the little atheist' (p. 5).

TEXT 3   (III, 5 PAGES 168–70)

> She looked now at the drawing-room step. She saw, through William's eyes, the shape of a woman, peaceful and silent, with downcast eyes. She sat musing, pondering (she was in grey that day, Lily thought). Her eyes were bent. She would never lift them. Yes, thought Lily, looking intently, I must have seen her look like that, but not in grey; nor so still, nor so young, nor so peaceful. The figure came readily enough. She was astonishingly beautiful, William said. But beauty was not everything. Beauty had this penalty – it came too readily, came too completely. It stilled life – froze it. One forgot the little agitations; the flush, the pallor, some queer distortion, some light or shadow, which made the face unrecognisable for a moment and yet added a quality one saw for ever after. It was simpler to smooth that all out under the cover of beauty. But what was the look she had, Lily wondered, when she clapped her deer-stalker's hat on her head, or ran across the grass, or scolded Kennedy, the gardener? Who could tell her? Who could help her?
>
> Against her will she had come to the surface, and found herself half out of the picture, looking, a little dazedly, as if at unreal things, at Mr Carmichael. He lay

on his chair with his hands clasped above his paunch not reading, or sleeping, but basking like a creature gorged with existence. His book had fallen on to the grass.

She wanted to go straight up to him and say, 'Mr Carmichael!' Then he would look up benevolently as always, from his smoky vague green eyes. But one only woke people if one knew what one wanted to say to them. And she wanted to say not one thing, but everything. Little words that broke up the thought and dismembered it said nothing. 'About life, about death; about Mrs Ramsay' – no, she thought, one could say nothing to nobody. The urgency of the moment always missed its mark. Words fluttered sideways and struck the object inches too low. Then one gave it up; then the idea sunk back again; then one became like most middle-aged people, cautious, furtive, with wrinkles between the eyes and a look of perpetual apprehension. For how could one express in words these emotions of the body? express that emptiness there? (She was looking at the drawing-room steps; they looked extraordinarily empty). It was one's body feeling, not one's mind. The physical sensations that went with the bare look of the steps had become suddenly extremely unpleasant. To want and not to have sent all up her body a hardness, a hollowness, a strain. And then to want and not to have – to want and want- how that wrung the heart, and wrung it again and again! Oh Mrs. Ramsay! she called out silently, to that essence which sat by the boat, that abstract one made of her, that woman in grey, as if to abuse her for having gone, and then having gone, come back again. It had seemed so safe, thinking of her. Ghost, air, nothingness, a thing you could play with easily and safely at any time of day or night, she had been that, and then suddenly she put her hand out and wrung the heart thus. Suddenly, the empty drawing-room steps, the frill of the chair inside, the puppy tumbling on the terrace, the whole wave and whisper of the garden became like curves and arabesques flourishing round the centre of complete emptiness.

We learn of Mrs Ramsay's death in the course of 'Time Passes'. In the novel's final section we see that she continues to exist, in a sense, in the memories of those who knew her. Lily Briscoe recognises the example Mrs Ramsay provided through her insistent attempts to create bridges between people. Through her painting, Lily manages to give objective form to the subjective awareness she had of that process of drawing together. In this passage she recalls her old friend, aware of her physical absence, yet intent on following through the lesson that was her most valuable legacy.

Lily envisages the shape of Mrs Ramsay as if through the eyes of William Bankes. This confirms the affection she feels for Bankes. It also demonstrates her ability to empathise with other points of view, her willingness to forgo a sense that her own self is privileged in its understanding of the world. This lack of shallow egotism is important to her success as an artist, engaging with the world on equal terms, rather than trying to impose some theory upon it.

Bankes comments upon the physical beauty which was noted by all who knew Mrs Ramsay, even as she grew older. Lily, perhaps conscious that she is not herself considered a beauty, comments upon the limitations of such perfection: 'It stilled life – froze it'. Beauty here appears sterile, like a philosophical model or a mathematical formula, perfect yet lacking vitality. Lily approaches her art, as Virginia Woolf did, as a means to realise balanced and coherent form, while incorporating the vitality of life as it is lived.

Kennedy the gardener is another employee of the Ramsay household. Although Bankes remarks that the family is not rich, the Ramsays are clearly comfortably off. Working-class figures do the physical work around their house. For example, although Mrs Ramsay feels triumphant at her dinner party in I, 17, the food was actually cooked by Mildred, a servant.

The notion of Lily coming to the surface may recall I, 11 where we saw Mrs Ramsay immersed in the depths of her being (see Textual Analysis – Text 2). Considering herself 'half out of the picture' is an appropriate **metaphor** for Lily's state of mind. A painting preoccupies her throughout the novel, and at the end she realises that she must be totally engaged with the picture to be able to complete it.

Virginia Woolf considers language inherently inadequate to express what it is really like to be in the world. In this passage, we have an explicit statement of that inadequacy. Verbal expression fragments reality: 'Little words that broke up the thought and dismembered it said nothing.' Lily wants to say 'not one thing, but everything'. But 'everything' is infinitely complex, and words consequently seem incredibly reductive. She concludes that 'one could say nothing to nobody'.

Lily and the other characters still strive to communicate, but at this moment she recognises that expression is often an empty pretence, a conventional formulation rather than genuine engagement with being alive. Overwhelmed by the question, 'how could one express in words these emotions of the body?', she remarks upon the polite formality and cliché that characterise the perpetually apprehensive middle-aged. Through her art Lily transcends these limitations and manages to say everything she needs to say. At this point, however, she is tormented by her desire for the return of Mrs Ramsay. She is haunted by the vacuum left by that woman's absence, pained by recollection of her. Completion of her picture at the end of the novel consoles her for that loss; it enables her to 'express that emptiness there'.

The presence of a puppy, 'tumbling on the terrace', may seem like an incidental detail, but it provides a link between Lily on land and the Ramsays on the boat. Mr Ramsay asks Cam questions about the dog in III, 4.

PART FIVE

BACKGROUND

VIRGINIA WOOLF

Virginia Woolf was born Adeline Virginia Stephen, on 25 January 1882. Her parents were Leslie and Julia Stephen. She had an older sister and brother, Vanessa and Thoby. A younger brother, Adrian, was born in October 1883. Both parents had been married previously; her father brought to the household a daughter, Laura, while George, Stella and Gerald Duckworth were the children of her mother's first marriage.

It was a large, late-Victorian, upper-middle-class family, and a literary household. Leslie Stephen was a well-known man of letters, whose life was devoted to studies in the history of philosophy, and to editorship of the *Dictionary of National Biography*. His first wife was the daughter of the famous novelist William Makepeace Thackeray (1811–63). Leslie Stephen died in 1904, following a long illness during which Virginia nursed him attentively. She admired her father as a dedicated writer, but recognised his capacity to be a tyrant. He provided a model for Mr Ramsay.

In 1881, Leslie Stephen bought a house at St Ives, in Cornwall. The family spent summer holidays there until 1895, when Julia Stephen died. Relocated far to the north in the British Isles, these holidays provided the basis for Virginia Woolf's account of the Ramsays. She regarded her mother, who provided a model for Mrs Ramsay, as a beautiful woman, whose calming influence presided over her childhood. But she recognised that Julia Stephen, conservative in her view of the social role of women, embodied the passivity of the stereotypical Victorian 'Angel of the House', in Coventry Patmore's phrase.

Following her mother's death, Virginia experienced a kind of nervous breakdown. Other breakdowns occurred at intervals throughout her life, and she came to fear a descent into madness. The traumatic loss of her mother was compounded by the death during pregnancy, in 1897, of her half-sister, Stella. This incident may be reflected in the manner of Prue Ramsay's death. In 1906, she experienced another harrowing loss when Thoby, her favourite brother, died of typhoid.

Her education was unsystematic. Her mother believed that her daughter should learn domestic management rather than engaging in intellectual pursuits. Her father had a substantial library and encouraged her to read extensively, but there was no prospect of her attending university as her brothers did.

By the end of 1904 she had started to publish journalistic pieces in the *Guardian*, and over the next five years she developed her writing skills in essays for the *Times Literary Supplement*, the *Cornhill* magazine, and other journals. She also travelled in Europe.

In 1907, her sister Vanessa married Clive Bell. Both became members of the Bloomsbury Group (see Literary Background). In 1909, a legacy from her aunt, Caroline Stephen, allowed Virginia to devote more of her time to writing novels. But although this was the course she wished her life to take, she experienced further mental illness. In 1912 she married Leonard Woolf, who gave up a job in the Colonial Civil Service in order to become her husband; nevertheless, in 1913 she made a serious attempt to commit suicide.

In 1917, the couple bought a small second-hand printing press, and before long the Hogarth Press was launched from the basement of their home in Richmond, Surrey. This development was of considerable importance to Virginia Woolf, as it granted her freedom to write as she pleased, without having to face the criticisms and interventions of publishing houses.

Throughout the 1930s, her reputation as a novelist grew, but the Woolfs viewed with anxiety the political situation in Europe. Their liberal values seemed threatened by the rise of Fascist dictatorships. War broke out in 1939. In 1941, while they were staying at their country home at Rodmell, Sussex, Virginia Woolf wrote letters to her sister and to her husband saying that she feared the onset of madness, from which she would not recover. She then drowned herself in the River Ouse.

Autobiographical revelations can be gleaned from the five volumes of *The Diary of Virginia Woolf*, edited by Anne Olivier Bell (Hogarth Press, 1977–84). The definitive biography is her nephew Quentin Bell's two-volume *Virginia Woolf: A Biography* (Hogarth Press, 1972). An intimate recollection of her can be found in Leonard Woolf's *An Autobiography* (Oxford University Press, 1980).

Recent biographies include: Phyllis Rose, *Woman of Letters: A Life of Virginia Woolf* (Routledge, 1978); Lyndall Gordon, *Virginia Woolf: A Writer's Life* (Oxford University Press, 1984); John Mepham, *Virginia Woolf: A Literary Life* (Macmillan, 1991); and Hermione Lee, *Virginia Woolf* (Chatto & Windus, 1996).

OTHER WORKS BY VIRGINIA WOOLF

Virginia Woolf's first novel, *The Voyage Out*, was published in 1915; a revised edition was published in 1920. *Night and Day* appeared in 1919, but it was in *Jacob's Room*, in 1922, that she first wrote in the innovative style that aligned her with the literary Modernists (see Literary Background – Modernism). She affirmed this alignment in her essay 'Mr Bennett and Mrs Brown' (1923).

Virginia Woolf's reputation as a major twentieth-century novelist rests upon the novels that followed. The action of *Mrs Dalloway* (1925), which is set in central London, takes place on a single day. The portrayal of Mrs Ramsay as a wife and mother is in some ways foreshadowed in the characterisation of Clarissa Dalloway, whose life is circumscribed by domestic obligations, and who acts similarly as a hostess. The novel marked a significant advance in Virginia Woolf's use of **stream of consciousness** technique. *Jacob's Room* was an anti-war novel: Jacob Flanders died fighting in the First World War. In *Mrs Dalloway*, a character named Septimus Warren-Smith has been driven insane by his experiences in that war. In neither case is the treatment of combat direct, but both convey Virginia Woolf's revulsion at the slaughter. The brutal reality of the war haunts 'Time Passes', the second part of *To the Lighthouse* (1927).

Orlando (1928) is lighter in tone. It is a tale of transformation, which follows the main character switching through time between male and female identities. Virginia Woolf's critical interest in conventional gender roles is to the fore. *The Waves* (1931) is Virginia Woolf's most challenging novel, dense and lyrical. Here she pursued **stream of consciousness** technique to a point where it tests the limits of the novel form.

In 1937, she published *The Years*, a family saga. It is written in more traditional style with more extensive external description, as if she recognised that *The Waves* had taken **stream of consciousness** to a point beyond which she could not venture. Virginia Woolf left behind at her death the manuscript of *Between the Acts* (1941). It portrays the staging of a historical pageant during the months before the Second World War, and ranks with her best fiction.

Virginia Woolf's critical essays are generally worthy of attention. *Collected Essays*, in four volumes, was published by Hogarth Press in 1966–7. Two longer essays have been published separately, and are important for an understanding of Virginia Woolf's feminism. *A Room of One's Own* (1929) is especially concerned with the prospects of women who wish to become writers. *Three Guineas* (1938), a response to the rise of Fascism in Europe, expounds her pacifist and feminist views, and asks what women might do to avoid further warfare. She argues that men are essentially immature, and that women must help them attain the maturity necessary for civilised existence.

HISTORICAL BACKGROUND

CONTEMPORARY PESSIMISM

'Progress' was a key word in British culture during the first part of the nineteenth century. There was popular faith that the power of scientific understanding and technological ingenuity, which had driven the Industrial Revolution in the mid eighteenth century, would continue to ensure a better standard of living for the entire population. Underpinning that belief was a strong Christian sense that steady improvement was part of God's benign plan. But the latter part of the nineteenth century saw a waning of Christian belief, especially amongst middle-class intellectuals, and faith in progress was eroded accordingly.

Particularly significant was the publication of *The Origin of Species* (1859) and *The Descent of Man* (1871) by Charles Darwin (1809–82). The theory of evolution expounded there undermined traditional understanding of the world and of the place of human beings within it. In *To the Lighthouse*, Mr Ramsay contemplates 'the long wastes of the ages' (p. 33), which had been disclosed by Darwin, and by the work of Victorian geologists. Mrs Ramsay momentarily puts her trust in a beneficent Lord, only to recant immediately, chastising herself for lapsing into that 'lie' (p. 59). More generally, Virginia Woolf's view of the world is clearly pervaded by fear of imminent chaos. In this she conformed to the pessimistic view that prevailed amongst intellectuals and artists during the early decades of the twentieth century. For many people, the First World War seemed a graphic denial of purpose or meaning, contributing to more widespread pessimism.

The first world war

The First World War, fought between 1914 and 1918, haunted Virginia Woolf's writing throughout the 1920s. She recognised that in this prolonged and gruesome conflict, fought between supposedly 'civilised' European powers, scientific knowledge and technological prowess were placed in the service of barbarism. Her pacifist views were reinforced by her feminist opposition to the patriarchal order, which she blamed for initiating and perpetuating the fighting. During the four years of the war, she experienced prolonged bouts of mental illness, and it seemed to her that her inner torment was mirrored by the suffering imposed on Europe as young men died and their families mourned. She was appalled by the mindlessness of popular patriotism, and the crassness of official rhetoric.

The general strike

The dominant social event that occurred in Britain at the time Virginia Woolf was writing *To the Lighthouse* was the General Strike, organised by the Labour movement in May 1926. As her diary entries show, Virginia Woolf followed this course of events with attentive concern. At the time she was engaged in writing 'Time Passes'. The turbulence of national unrest and class conflict is perhaps registered in the instability and decay that informs that part of the novel. The figure of Mrs McNab was conceived at a time when Virginia Woolf was acutely aware of the demanding physicality of working-class life, while also aware of the remoteness from those circumstances of her own privileged position. Her sympathy with working-class families enduring hardship was coupled with distaste for the discomfort brought about by the strike, and anxiety concerning the uncertain prospects for her own class if the action were successful. In fact, the collective Labour effort soon collapsed leaving the miners to continue the diminished campaign in isolation.

LITERARY BACKGROUND

EDWARDIAN FICTION

In her essay 'Mr Bennett and Mrs Brown', Virginia Woolf contrasted her own imaginative characterisation of a woman observed on a train with the portrayal that might be expected from Arnold Bennett, H.G. Wells and John Galsworthy. These novelists, all popular during the Edwardian period (1901–11), she termed 'Materialists', because they concentrated on external description and neglected the inner life of their characters. Like their Victorian precursors, they attempted a panoramic view of the society of their day. Virginia Woolf rejected this broad sweep, preferring to focus upon the intimate details of individual lives.

The fiction of Wells, Galsworthy and Bennett proceeds from the assumption that characters and communities can be known, and that such knowledge may be conveyed straightforwardly through the medium of language. Virginia Woolf aligned herself instead with the literary Modernists, whose work often takes as its central concern the struggle towards some form of knowing, rather than achieved knowledge.

MODERNISM

Modernism is a term that has been applied to a wide range of literary, artistic and musical works, mostly produced during the first three decades of the twentieth century. They have in common a self-conscious dedication to formal and technical innovation, usually linked to a sense that reality is too elusive and contradictory to be rendered through conventional representation.

Bennett, Wells and Galsworthy came in for cutting criticism in 'Mr Bennett and Mrs Brown'. Praise was reserved there for novelists seeking to do something different, to acknowledge that character is far less stable, fixed and self-evident than the previous generation would concede. The new writers included E.M. Forster, D.H. Lawrence and

James Joyce. Although Virginia Woolf had serious reservations about the subject matter of James Joyce's novel *Ulysses* (1922), which she found too frank in its treatment of bodily functions, she admired and learnt from Joyce's technical virtuosity. She also drew lessons from the short stories of Katherine Mansfield, and the stream of consciousness fiction written by Dorothy Richardson.

THE BLOOMSBURY GROUP

The 'Bloomsbury Group' was a loose and eclectic affiliation of artists and intellectuals based in the area around the British Museum in London, where Vanessa and Virginia Stephen had a house. It achieved public prominence through the presence in the group of figures such as novelist E.M. Forster, economist John Maynard Keynes, painter Roger Fry and writer Lytton Strachey. Fry organised the first exhibition of Post-Impressionist paintings in England in 1910, championing French innovation against the conservatism of the British art establishment. Lytton Strachey's *Eminent Victorians* (1918) was a deliberate attempt to undermine the monumental authority that had become attached to representative Victorian figures.

A good introduction can be found in *A Bloomsbury Group Reader*, edited by S.P. Rosenbaum (Blackwell, 1993).

PART SIX

C RITICAL HISTORY &
BROADER PERSPECTIVES

R ECEPTION AND CRITICAL HISTORY

To the Lighthouse has been widely regarded as Virginia Woolf's finest novel. Initial reviews were generally supportive of her ambitiousness, if at times bemused by the result. Arnold Bennett, in the *Evening Standard* (23 June 1927), and Edwin Muir in the *Nation and Atheneum* (2 July 1927) both suggested that 'Time Passes' was less successful than the other parts of the novel. A critic writing for the *Monthly Criterion* (July 1927) argued that the term 'novel' did not properly fit a prose work of this kind, which at times approaches poetry.

In 1928, *To the Lighthouse* was awarded the *Prix Femina*, established by the French *Vie Heureuse* magazine. Critical acclaim was matched by encouraging sales. During the 1930s, however, adverse criticism surfaced from members of the *Scrutiny* group surrounding the influential academic critic F.R. Leavis. They argued that in its intense focus upon the individual Virginia Woolf's fiction neglected important social and political realities. Winifred Holtby spoke in her defence in her early study, *Virginia Woolf* (Wishart, London, 1932).

Virginia Woolf's death in 1941 prompted further reassessment. David Daiches identified *To the Lighthouse* as the 'perfection' of Virginia Woolf's art in his *Virginia Woolf* (New Directions, New York, 1942). Joan Bennett, in *Virginia Woolf: Her art as a novelist* (Cambridge University Press, 1945), wrote of her as an author misunderstood because she placed sympathy with her characters before critical judgement of them.

An important landmark in serious criticism of *To the Lighthouse* was Erich Auerbach's analysis of Virginia Woolf's use of multiple point of view, and her treatment of time, in the concluding chapter of his classic study, *Mimesis: The Representation of Reality in Western Literature* (Princeton University Press, 1953; first published in Switzerland, 1946). His example fostered a prominent strand of criticism analysing Virginia Woolf's narrative techniques.

In 1953, the Marxist critic Arnold Kettle, in *An Introduction to the English Novel* (Hutchinson, London, 1961; first published 1953) praised

Virginia Woolf's skill, yet dismissed the novel, which he considered trivial. Less politically directed critical work during the 1960s developed exploration of the novel's symbolism, and investigated its links with painting. A selection of criticism written prior to 1970, including pieces by Leavis, Kettle, Auerbach and Daiches can be found in *Twentieth Century Interpretations of To the Lighthouse*, edited by Thomas A. Vogler (Prentice-Hall, 1970).

Quentin Bell's biography of Virginia Woolf appeared in 1972. Later in the decade, her letters and diaries were published. Together these materials constituted a resource that stimulated new angles of critical investigation, especially of a psychological nature. Louise de Salvo produced a controversial landmark in biographical criticism with her *Virginia Woolf: The Impact of Childhood Sexual Abuse on her Life and Work* (The Women's Press, London, 1989). Quentin Bell's biography had disclosed that Virginia Woolf endured abuse as a child from the Duckworth brothers.

Feminist criticism of the novel has been prolific and productive during the past quarter of a century. Jane Marcus has edited two important volumes: *New Feminist Essays on Virginia Woolf* (Macmillan, London, 1981) and *Virginia Woolf: A Feminist Slant* (University of Nebraska Press, Lincoln, 1983). These books set an agenda for current work on Virginia Woolf which, by placing particular emphasis upon Virginia Woolf's own feminism, attempts to show that her work is politically responsible in ways not recognised by earlier critics, such as F.R. Leavis and Arnold Kettle.

CONTEMPORARY APPROACHES

FREUDIAN CRITICISM

The theories of psychoanalysis developed by Sigmund Freud (1856–1939) became fashionable during the early decades of the twentieth century, but Virginia Woolf regarded them with caution. She feared that Freud's explanatory system would prove a reductive model, oversimplifying the complex nature of human beings. Subsequent criticism of Freud's work has challenged the patriarchal assumptions that underlie many of his arguments, but psychoanalytic criticism can still provide stimulating perspectives upon literary works.

Freud's vital contribution to psychology was his theory of the dynamic unconscious. He argued that human beings are susceptible to impulses which, if they were acted upon, would cause the self to disintegrate and society to collapse. These impulses are predominantly sexual or aggressive. Through a process Freud termed repression, dangerous urges are consigned to the unconscious, which can never be known directly by the conscious mind. Importantly, these repressed elements need to find an outlet of some kind. They may surface as symptoms of mental illness, or they may appear as slips of the tongue as we speak. They may be 'sublimated' through artistic expression, or they may form the stuff of our dreams. There are other modes of release.

The unconscious is never known directly, and it influences our behaviour in ways of which we are unaware. In *The Interpretation of Dreams* (1900), Freud suggested that dreams involve a kind of symbolic language which translates unconscious elements into recognisable forms. It is possible to make a coherent reading of *To the Lighthouse* in terms of Freudian symbolism. The Lighthouse itself may be regarded as a 'phallic symbol', underlining the masculine authority that presides, in the novel, over external reality. It stands in isolation, yet is an object of desire, and one of the most significant moments in the book occurs when Mrs Ramsay experiences a sense of communion with its beam. We might see this as a symbolic form of sexual coupling.

Sexuality and aggression are combined in the knives and scimitars associated with Mr Ramsay. These penetrative objects may also suggest phallic symbolism, casting light on some underlying motivation for Ramsay's overbearing, tyrannical behaviour. On the other hand, the stocking that his wife knits can be seen in Freudian terms as symbolic of female sexuality. It is receptive and passive, yet offers protection to its wearer.

Jasper's gun may be seen as a further example of phallic symbolism, revealing the destructive potential of masculine desire to dominate and control. Cam feels threatened by the boar's skull, with its protruding tusks, on her bedroom wall, while James derives pleasure from it. Minta Doyle's fear of bulls, also horned animals, perhaps suggests her anxiety at the imminent prospect of a mature sexual relationship. On the other hand, Mr Ramsay casually taps out his pipe on a ram's horn that forms the handle of an urn, the symbolism suggesting that the sexualised world holds no fears for this father of eight.

This pattern of symbols may seem to suggest that Virginia Woolf's characterisation endorses a view that men are naturally active and aggressive, while women are naturally passive and accommodating. But if Mr Ramsay is lean as a knife, Mr Carmichael has a 'capacious paunch' (p. 9) as if pregnant with his own creativity; and if Mrs Ramsay carries a basket, Lily Briscoe brandishes a paintbrush as if appropriating phallic potency for her creative ends. Art may be seen, through this symbolism, to offer an antidote to the menace and overt violence of the masculine social order, and to the compliance that follows from female acceptance and passivity.

One of Sigmund Freud's most controversial theories, outlined in his *General Theory of Psychoanalysis* (1916), is known as the Oedipus complex. In a classical Greek tragedy, written by Sophocles (*c.*496–406BC), the character Oedipus unknowingly murders his father and marries his mother. Freud argued that comparable repressed impulses shape the development of male behaviour. The violent response of James Ramsay to his father at the start of the novel, and his evident affection for his mother might be seen in the light of this complex. There is some evidence within the text to support the view that Virginia Woolf was making conscious use of this concept. In III, 8 James, musing on his relationship with his father, suddenly envisages an image of a damaged foot (p. 176). Oedipus was given his Greek name, which means Swell-Foot, because as a baby his ankles were pinned before he was abandoned on a mountainside.

A more sophisticated example of the psychoanalytical approach can be found in Rachel Bowlby's *Virginia Woolf: Feminist Destinations* (Basil Blackwell, Oxford, 1988).

MARXIST CRITICISM

This approach reads literary works in the light of the model of history and of the political and economic analysis elaborated in the writings of the German philosopher, Karl Marx (1818–83). Marxist criticism pays particular attention to the relationship between social classes within a literary work. Its central tenet is that the action of an entire class determines the course of history. Individuals are seen as products of a particular class within society as a whole, rather than as self-sufficient beings.

Unsurprisingly, Virginia Woolf's fiction has met with a broadly hostile reception from Marxist critics. They favour novels that reflect collective experience, and reveal historical forces at work. Virginia Woolf focused upon the minutiae of daily experience and the nuances of individual perception. *To the Lighthouse* engages sympathetically with the life of an upper middle-class family, which can afford a holiday home and is able to employ servants. Marx saw the working class as the driving force for the next stage of social evolution. But in this novel, that class is represented by the coarse and witless figure of Mrs McNab. A Marxist critic would see her characterisation as evidence of bourgeois condescension on Virginia Woolf's part.

Charles Tansley also has a working-class background, but he has striven to advance himself through education. Marxist criticism would point out that Virginia Woolf depicts him as riddled with anxiety and uncertainty as a consequence of his entry into a middle-class social circle. He is not an agent of change, but is himself diluted and embittered. In that light the Ramsays may also be seen as representatives of a class that has lost confidence in itself and in the world around it. Mr and Mrs Ramsay live in a climate of fear, symptomatic of the bourgeoisie in its decadence. Mr Ramsay worries about the fishermen and their wages. Mrs Ramsay is concerned to improve the sanitation and health of the poor. But in Marxist terms these are superficial responses to deeply rooted problems which require a revolutionary response rather than piecemeal reform.

In the Marxist view, art should be an agent of such revolutionary change. Lily Briscoe's painting clearly fails to meet this requirement. It is a highly personal work, probably destined to be stored away or (condescendingly) to be hung in a servant's room. It will not engage with historical reality in a direct and purposeful way, and its obliqueness, like that of *To the Lighthouse*, would be taken by a Marxist as a sign of its impotence to effect social change. This criticism assumes additional pungency from the fact that in May 1926, when Virginia Woolf was writing the book, a General Strike, organised by the British Labour movement, seemed for a short while to pose a serious challenge to the established social order.

The Marxist critic Arnold Kettle, after praising the 'luminous' quality of *To the Lighthouse,* and conceding that Virginia Woolf's characters seem 'alive', declared that the novel is not about anything very interesting or important. He found it inconsequential on account of the absence of 'a framework of human effort', and called into question the significance of Lily Briscoe's achievement in having her vision and completing her painting. His comments may be found in *Twentieth Century Interpretations of To the Lighthouse,* edited by Thomas A. Vogler (Prentice-Hall, 1970).

FEMINIST CRITICISM

Virginia Woolf articulated her own feminist position in the extended essays *A Room of One's Own* (1929) and *Three Guineas* (1938). Feminism has subsequently developed a range of sophisticated approaches to reading literary works. Some might be critical of Virginia Woolf's narrow focus upon the concerns of middle-class women. The inner lives of Mrs Ramsay and Lily Briscoe are revealed in meticulous detail. Mrs McNab, the caretaker, on the other hand, is crudely rendered as a coarse gossip. Despite this possible shortcoming, however, feminist readings have recognised the importance of Virginia Woolf's critical treatment of patriarchal values, which she saw as repressive and ultimately destructive.

Virginia Woolf depicts Mr Ramsay as a tyrannical embodiment of masculine assumptions, while his wife, for all her positive qualities, is limited by her acceptance of the allocated roles of wife and mother. Lily Briscoe, rejecting domestic confinement, pursues her own goals as an artist. In doing so, she absorbs lessons learnt from observation of the older woman's strengths, while affirming her independence from the values of male domination. She continues to paint despite the friendly incomprehension of William Bankes and the overt hostility of Charles Tansley, who believes that women can make no contribution to art. Additionally, we know that Mr Ramsay regards art as a mere embellishment. However, Mrs Ramsay also fails to appreciate the value of Lily's activity. That blind spot in itself indicates the need for an assertion of feminist aesthetics of the kind Virginia Woolf offers in *A Room of One's Own*.

There is more than narrowly aesthetic value at stake in *To the Lighthouse*. A feminist critic might argue that conventional historical accounts of the First World War, written in a factual and analytic style of the kind favoured by the patriarchal Mr Ramsay, fail to convey the value of the lives sacrificed in the slaughter. Virginia Woolf's approach to writing, which attends to intimate details and highly personal sensations while investigating how these subjective experiences mesh to form collective understanding, may be seen as a technical and stylistic challenge to patriarchal modes of comprehension.

Reading Virginia Woolf's novel you necessarily engage in a different way of knowing the world than is required by a conventional history book. So although the war is mentioned only fleetingly, in connection with Andrew Ramsay's death, we have a strongly developed sense of what is lost. An entire world located within that young man's consciousness has been bluntly extinguished. The loss reverberates traumatically through the consciousness of each person left behind who knew him. The statistical record favoured by patriarchal discourse has been displaced by the insight permitted by a woman's writing.

Feminist criticism might point to the fluency and expansiveness of Virginia Woolf's prose as a corrective to patriarchal writing, which is insistently linear, like Mr Ramsay's mind plodding through the letters of the alphabet. Mrs Ramsay and Lily share a concern for wholeness, for unified understanding of a kind that has been shattered by the analytical habits of masculine intelligence. Women, excluded from public power, have preserved a capacity for synthesis which is socially marginalised by patriarchal determination to dissect and classify.

A feminist reading might show how that marginalisation resulted in the blinkered vision which precipitated the horrors of the First World War. It was an outrage initiated by men, and fought amongst them. Virginia Woolf saw it as the nadir of patriarchal brutishness. *To the Lighthouse* appears, in a responsive feminist reading, as a step to assert another set of values and another order of cultural and social priorities. The fact that it does not appear to be politically engaged is actually an indication that the novel is fully operative within an alternative politics of gender.

Jane Marcus has made major contributions to feminist writing on Virginia Woolf. She has edited *New Feminist Essays on Virginia Woolf* (Basingstoke, 1981), and *Virginia Woolf: A Feminist Slant* (University of Nebraska Press, Lincoln, 1983), and is author of *Virginia Woolf and the Languages of Patriarchy* (Indiana University Press, Bloomington, 1987).

World events		Virginia Woolf	Literary context
	1921		*Crome Yellow* by Aldous Huxley
Tomb of ancient Egyptian King, Tutankhamun, discovered by Howard Carter	**1922**	Novel, *Jacob's Room*	*Ulysses* by James Joyce
	1923	Essay, 'Mr Bennett and Mrs Brown' published in *Nation and the Athenaeum*	*Whose Life?* by Dorothy L. Sayers
	1924		*A Passage to India* by E.M. Forster
			The Magic Mountain by Thomas Mann
	1925	Novel, *Mrs Dalloway*	*The Great Gatsby* by F. Scott Fitzgerald
			Manhattan Transfer by John Dos Passos
			The Counterfeiters by André Gide
General Strike in Britain	**1926**		*The Castle* by Franz Kafka
	1927	**To the Lighthouse published**	Final part of *A la recherche du temps perdu* by Marcel Proust published posthumously

World events		Virginia Woolf	Literary context
	1927 continued		*Steppenwolf* by Hermann Hesse
Equal Franchise Act gives women over twenty-one the vote in Britain	**1928**	Novel, *Orlando* *To the Lighthouse* wins the Prix Femina	*Lady Chatterley's Lover* by D.H. Lawrence printed privately in Italy *Decline and Fall* by Evelyn Waugh
	1929	Extended essay, *A Room of One's Own*	*The Sound and the Fury* by William Faulkner *A Farewell to Arms* by Ernest Hemingway
	1930		*The Edwardians* by Vita Sackville-West *Cakes and Ale* by W. Somerset Maugham
	1931	Novel, *The Waves*	*Men and Wives* by Ivy Compton-Burnett
	1932		*Journey to the End of the Night* by Ferdinand Céline *Cold Comfort Farm* by Stella Gibbons *Brave New World* by Aldous Huxley

caricature grotesque rendering of character, achieved through exaggeration of distinctive traits

elegy a poetical lamentation

figurative language any form of expression that departs from the basic requirements of simple communication, especially through the employment of metaphor

flashback a term borrowed from cinema, indicating a leap backwards to a scene or event that occurred earlier than the present action

free indirect style a blending of first- and third-person narration, which grants access to a character's thoughts, while preserving a certain detachment

interior monologue technique for depicting the workings of an individual character's consciousness

irony saying one thing but meaning another. This often involves an ostensible or intended meaning being altered by the context

metaphor describing one thing as being another thing in order to highlight a particular quality which both share

metonymy referring to a thing by means of an attribute it possesses or by a quality associated with it

motif some element, such as a particular image or a characteristic phrase, which recurs frequently within a literary work

myth a mode of understanding reality that transcends those particularities of time and space with which history is concerned. Myth consequently tends to refer to the activities of superhuman beings

parenthesis material placed between brackets and inserted into a passage so that it simultaneously appears part of and distinct from that passage

parody an imitation of a particular work or of a type of literature, usually, but not invariably, making fun of its characteristic features

personification figurative device that treats things or ideas as if they possessed human qualities

plot not simply a story, but the conscious arrangement of its components in order to tell it in a particular way pun a play on words, reliant upon recognition of more than one meaning attaching to a single word

realism or realist fiction fiction that proceeds from the assumption that characters and communities can be known, and that such knowledge may be conveyed through the medium of language. Modernist literature, contrastingly, often takes the struggle towards some form of knowing, rather than achieved knowledge as its central concern

simile a kind of metaphorical writing in which one thing is said to be like another thing

story a tellable sequence of events

stream of consciousness narrative technique, exemplified by *To the Lighthouse*, employing a narrative voice that is able to pass from one character's consciousness to another, tracing in detail the processes of thought, sensory perception and emotional states

symbol an image that represents something else

AUTHOR OF THIS NOTE

Dr Julian Cowley taught English at King's College London before joining the University of Luton, where he is Senior Lecturer in Literary Studies.

Notes

York Notes Advanced (£3.99 each)

Margaret Atwood
Cat's Eye

Margaret Atwood
The Handmaid's Tale

Jane Austen
Mansfield Park

Jane Austen
Persuasion

Jane Austen
Pride and Prejudice

Alan Bennett
Talking Heads

William Blake
Songs of Innocence and of Experience

Charlotte Brontë
Jane Eyre

Emily Brontë
Wuthering Heights

Angela Carter
Nights at the Circus

Geoffrey Chaucer
The Franklin's Tale

Geoffrey Chaucer
The Miller's Prologue and Tales

Geoffrey Chaucer
Prologue To the Canterbury Tales

Geoffrey Chaucer
The Wife of Bath's Prologue and Tale

Joseph Conrad
Heart of Darkness

Charles Dickens
Great Expectations

Charles Dickens
Hard Times

Emily Dickinson
Selected Poems

John Donne
Selected Poems

Carol Ann Duffy
Selected Poems

George Eliot
Middlemarch

George Eliot
The Mill on the Floss

T.S. Eliot
Selected Poems

F. Scott Fitzgerald
The Great Gatsby

E.M. Forster
A Passage to India

Brian Friel
Translations

Thomas Hardy
The Mayor of Casterbridge

Thomas Hardy
The Return of the Native

Thomas Hardy
Selected Poems

Thomas Hardy
Tess of the d'Urbervilles

Seamus Heaney
Selected Poems from Opened Ground

Nathaniel Hawthorne
The Scarlet Letter

Kazou Ishiguro
The Remains of the Day

James Joyce
Dubliners

John Keats
Selected Poems

Christopher Marlowe
Doctor Faustus

Arthur Miller
Death of a Salesman

John Milton
Paradise Lost Books I & II

Toni Morrison
Beloved

William Shakespeare
Antony and Cleopatra

William Shakespeare
As You Like It

William Shakespeare
Hamlet

William Shakespeare
King Lear

William Shakespeare
Measure for Measure

William Shakespeare
The Merchant of Venice

William Shakespeare
A Midsummer Night's Dream

William Shakespeare
Much Ado About Nothing

William Shakespeare
Othello

William Shakespeare
Richard II

William Shakespeare
Romeo and Juliet

William Shakespeare
The Taming of the Shrew

William Shakespeare
The Tempest

William Shakespeare
The Winter's Tale

George Bernard Shaw
Saint Joan

Mary Shelley
Frankenstein

Alice Walker
The Color Purple

Oscar Wilde
The Importance of Being Earnest

Tennessee Williams
A Streetcar Named Desire

John Webster
The Duchess of Malfi

Virginia Woolf
To the Lighthouse

W.B. Yeats
Selected Poems

GCSE and equivalent levels (£3.50 each)

Maya Angelou
I Know Why the Caged Bird Sings

Jane Austen
Pride and Prejudice

Alan Ayckbourn
Absent Friends

Elizabeth Barrett Browning
Selected Poems

Robert Bolt
A Man for All Seasons

Harold Brighouse
Hobson's Choice

Charlotte Brontë
Jane Eyre

Emily Brontë
Wuthering Heights

Shelagh Delaney
A Taste of Honey

Charles Dickens
David Copperfield

Charles Dickens
Great Expectations

Charles Dickens
Hard Times

Charles Dickens
Oliver Twist

Roddy Doyle
Paddy Clarke Ha Ha Ha

George Eliot
Silas Marner

George Eliot
The Mill on the Floss

William Golding
Lord of the Flies

Oliver Goldsmith
She Stoops To Conquer

Willis Hall
The Long and the Short and the Tall

Thomas Hardy
Far from the Madding Crowd

Thomas Hardy
The Mayor of Casterbridge

Thomas Hardy
Tess of the d'Urbervilles

Thomas Hardy
The Withered Arm and other Wessex Tales

L.P. Hartley
The Go-Between

Seamus Heaney
Selected Poems

Susan Hill
I'm the King of the Castle

Barry Hines
A Kestrel for a Knave

Louise Lawrence
Children of the Dust

Harper Lee
To Kill a Mockingbird

Laurie Lee
Cider with Rosie

Arthur Miller
The Crucible

Arthur Miller
A View from the Bridge

Robert O'Brien
Z for Zachariah

Frank O'Connor
My Oedipus Complex and other stories

George Orwell
Animal Farm

J.B. Priestley
An Inspector Calls

Willy Russell
Educating Rita

Willy Russell
Our Day Out

J.D. Salinger
The Catcher in the Rye

William Shakespeare
Henry IV Part 1

William Shakespeare
Henry V

William Shakespeare
Julius Caesar

William Shakespeare
Macbeth

William Shakespeare
The Merchant of Venice

William Shakespeare
A Midsummer Night's Dream

William Shakespeare
Much Ado About Nothing

William Shakespeare
Romeo and Juliet

William Shakespeare
The Tempest

William Shakespeare
Twelfth Night

George Bernard Shaw
Pygmalion

Mary Shelley
Frankenstein

R.C. Sherriff
Journey's End

Rukshana Smith
Salt on the snow

John Steinbeck
Of Mice and Men

Robert Louis Stevenson
Dr Jekyll and Mr Hyde

Jonathan Swift
Gulliver's Travels

Robert Swindells
Daz 4 Zoe

Mildred D. Taylor
Roll of Thunder, Hear My Cry

Mark Twain
Huckleberry Finn

James Watson
Talking in Whispers

William Wordsworth
Selected Poems

A Choice of Poets

Mystery Stories of the Nineteenth Century including The Signalman

Nineteenth Century Short Stories

Poetry of the First World War

Six Women Poets